THE HOUSE OF THE GODS

DAVIDE MANA

SEVERED PRESS
HOBART TASMANIA

THE HOUSE OF THE GODS

Copyright © 2017 Davide Mana

WWW.SEVEREDPRESS.COM

ISBN: 978-1-925711-55-4

For my brother

"There can be no doubt that the existing Fauna and Flora is but the last term of a long series of equally numerous contemporary species, which have succeeded one another, by the slow and gradual substitution of species for species, in the vast interval of time which has elapsed between the deposition of the earliest fossiliferous strata and the present day."

— Thomas Henry Huxley, *The Advance of Science in the Last Half-Century* (1887)

"It was surely well for man that he came late in the order of creation. There were powers abroad in earlier days which no courage and no mechanism of his could have met. What could his sling, his throwing-stick, or his arrow avail him against such forces as have been loose tonight? Even with a modern rifle it would be all odds on the monster."

— Arthur Conan Doyle, *The Lost World* (1912)

"Extinction is the rule. Survival is the exception."

— Carl Sagan, *The Varieties of Scientific Experience* (2006)

PART I

CHAPTER 1

A small, white metal arrow flying over the infinite green expanse of the Amazon jungle, the Pilatus PC-12 raced the storm, black clouds in hot pursuit. Lightning flashed through the boiling mass. It was a lost race. The plane fought to climb while the tempest rolled forward. A thin gray line of mountains loomed over the horizon, a broken rampart signaling the approaching boundary between Brazil and Venezuela.

"I say we go back," Rosita Nakajima said.

Mike glanced at his second pilot. They both knew it was only a matter of time before the storm would close over them. "Heading straight for the eye of the storm?"

Rosita was not convinced. "We can try and reach São Gabriel," she said. Without waiting for his reply, she picked up her pad and started browsing the maps.

"We will keep course," he said. He respected Rosita's skills, but they often did not see eye to eye. And this was his plane anyway. His plane, his company, his mortgage. "I'm staying out of that brew as long as I can."

Even if it looked like the ominous brew had a mind of its own, and quite other ideas.

The Pilatus, Mike's company's only asset, had done this route a thousand times in the last five years. Called Sligo Air in honor of his ancestor's home, his was one of the many small-time charter companies that handled the low-tier traffic over the Amazon and between Pacific and Atlantic oceans. Glorified bush pilots, the men and women who flew these routes were a closed community, and one that had its own rules. You make your choices, you take your responsibilities. Mike O'Reilly was the master and commander of his little bird, and his decision was final.

Rosita observed him. He looked tired and haggard, his short graying hair and his patchy beard giving him the look of a stray cat. Of a *sick* stray cat, she thought, wearing a crumpled khaki shirt.

Catching her glance, Mike grunted and made a show of concentrating on flying. She knew, just like he did, that an unscheduled stop, even if more than justified by the weather, would mean a penalty. And they could not afford to pay twenty percent on the engagement for the delay and the passengers' inconvenience. Their bank account was so empty it echoed, and the last thing they needed was to be blacklisted by tour operators and travel agents. The mountains were now a brown brushstroke in the distance, beyond the blur of the propeller. If they could make it to the mountains, they would be out of trouble. He settled more comfortably in his chair and perfunctorily checked the instruments.

"What about Tama-Tama?" she asked.

She did some quick distance and fuel calculations on her old-fashioned round slide rule. She had learned the old way, and the old way was fine with her. Tama-Tama could be close enough. They could spend the night there and let the storm roll over them. Better broke and blacklisted than killed in a freak storm over the Amazon, she told herself. That would be much worse for business.

Mike stared at the mountains for a few heartbeats.

"We keep course, we keep climbing," he said, finally. "As soon as we are over those rocks, we'll be clear."

Rosita sighed, flipping closed her clipboard. "It's your funeral," she said, resigned.

The petite Japanese-Peruvian woman with a pilot's license was getting tired of Mike's machismo. Wasn't she the one that was supposed to have a chip on her shoulder?

"Go check the passengers," he said.

"Afraid they'll jump ship?"

But she pushed back her seat and stood. Mike watched the mountains as they got closer, trying to ignore what the weather radar kept telling him.

#

Rosita made a quick stop in the closet-like lavatory, splashed some water on her face, straightened her blouse. Might as well look the part of the flight assistant. And who cared about her qualifications and experience after five years of commercial flying. She checked the passenger list: tourists and business people, the usual mix for a Sligo Air flight. Sligo Air being Mike back there at the controls, and his second mortgage used to buy this plane and keep it flying.

She sighed and pulled open the thick velvet curtain that separated the small service area from the executive-style passenger compartment. The Pilatus had been the house plane of a fish brokering company in Lima. The execs had flown it around when they went to the United States or Rio de Janeiro, to discuss the price of sardines. When the company had gone belly-up in the crash of 2009, Mike had bought the plane on the cheap and preserved the cabin layout. He said it gave the bird a touch of extra class.

Four of the seats faced each other across small wooden tables. The fittings were all polished wood and cream-colored upholstery where it counted, giving an impression of luxury. Their clients appreciated it. There were sockets for the laptops and the chairs had a wide, comfortable design.

Rosita had to stoop to walk along the aisle, the ceiling too low even for her short stature. She kept her balance by pushing a hand against the top.

A kid of maybe twenty with long blond hair and a Big Bang Theory T-shirt sat with his feet up against the bulwark, the print of the soles of his designer sneakers on the fine-grained wood paneling. He checked her out, grinned and gave her a hang-loose sign. He looked like Shaggy from Scooby-Doo.

"Where's the drink tray?" he said.

"Sit straight," she snapped, feeling like a spinster teacher. "We are going through some turbulence. You may want to fasten your seatbelt."

There were three of them, BBT guy, his girlfriend and a chum of theirs, a big guy in a football jersey. Americans, on one of the off-season, last-minute adventure package tours that made up the bulk of Mike's income these days. *Turistas* as they were known up and down the coast, and all through the once virgin forest. Rich kids in search of a thrill, blind to nature's beauty, too busy taking selfies.

Rosita shuddered inwardly. She was starting to think like an old woman, embracing the same prejudices her father used to have. She was still young. She felt she should feel some form of solidarity with the kids, but looking at this guy with his feet up against the wall, she realized she was not that young anymore. Not where it counted.

The kid took his feet down, eyeing her with an insouciant grin. Rosita sighed and advanced along the aisle. She glanced at the girl she had marked as BBT's girlfriend. Auburn hair, tight-fitting jeans and a tie-dyed T-shirt. She sat on the executive couch, busy ignoring the rest of the universe as she played with her smartphone, a morose look on her pretty face. *Trouble in paradise*, Rosita thought.

A long vibration ran through the plane, and Rosita felt like the floor was dropping away from under her. Air pocket. The beefy friend of BBT let out a loud whoop, and the two kids laughed out loud, high fiving across the aisle. The kids could not be more than five or six years her junior, but she felt a generation older. *I wasn't this stupid when I was in college*, she thought. The girl pouted some more and did her best to ignore her companions.

#

The plane shuddered, a long, unpleasant vibration running through the hull, a sound like an animal growl overcoming the drone of the engine. With the sound came the brief, unpleasant sensation of dropping. The kids in the front couches howled and slapped hands.

Sandra Barillier looked up from the pages of the *New England Journal of Medicine*. Focusing on the latest finds about Chikungunya and its prophylaxis was hard enough without the noise. And, as usual with medical texts, she was feeling the symptoms: joint and muscle pain, fatigue. Self-suggestion. A placebo effect in reverse.

The kids kept laughing and making a racket. The Japanese woman pilot was looking at them with an expression of pity.

Sandra had a novel in her carry-on but felt too lazy to take it out. Outside the window, dark clouds churned and boiled, the color of a bad bruise. The infinite expanse of green below had shifted from emerald to dark olive as the thunderstorms stole the sunshine. She placed her magazine on the small table. The big man sitting in front of her had his eyes closed. He wore a multi-pocket fishing vest over an aloha shirt. He breathed slowly and deeply in a deliberate way, his hands pressed on the table, a faint halo of perspiration surrounding his spread fingers on the polished surface.

"Fear of flying?" she asked, her bedside manners kicking in. Think about somebody else's discomfort to forget yours, was the principle.

The man did not react.

"Claustrophobia," a voice said by her side.

She turned. On the couch across the aisle, a thin, bald young man with a salt and pepper beard grinned at her, putting down a thick paperback. A girl sat in front of him, deeply entranced by whatever was happening on her phone.

"My brother can't stand closed spaces," the man said. He rubbed his hand on the front of his jean shirt and then offered it to her. "James Tanner. Jack." He nodded at the big man. "Meet my brother Steve, currently meditating his stress away."

She shook the hand. His skin was dry; the palm, calloused; the grip, firm. "Sandra Barillier."

"She is a doctor with the emergency organization," Steve Tanner said, opening his eyes. They were brown, just like his hair. It was the only thing the big man seemed to have in common with his brother. That and his affable grin. Sandra touched the emergency pin on the lapel of her safari jacket. "Currently on her way to Venezuela to settle some pretty non-medical issues with the French consulate."

He rubbed his hand on the front of his shirt, just like his brother had, and then extended it. She arched an eyebrow as she shook his hand. "You are very observant, Mister Tanner. A Sherlock fan?"

"Call me Steve. Mister Tanner was our father. You have met Jack." Steve looked out of the window and grimaced. "And I honestly can't stand the current takes on Holmes," he said, looking at her again. "I'm a Basil Rathbone fan. Nigel Bruce as Watson was wonderful. And as for my powers of deductions, I heard you in Fonte Boa when you were on your phone. You were talking pretty loud, you know."

"Some problems with management," Sandra said self-consciously.

The bearded man, Jack, grinned. "Better when he was meditating, innit?"

"There's always problems with management," Steve said. "You have my sympathy, for what it's worth."

"Everything fine, doctor?" the second pilot asked, stopping by. "Gentlemen?"

"Yes," she said, smiling at the Japanese woman. "We are fine."

The guys nodded in turn, Steve's smile maybe a little tight.

"You should buckle up," the woman said. Just then, the "fasten your seatbelts" sign went on with a loud ping.

"See?" she said.

"Glad to see you and the captain are on the same page," Steve quipped.

The Japanese woman smiled. "Yeah, it's reassuring, isn't it? Please fold the table, too."

"What brings you to the skies of the Amazon, gentlemen?" Sandra asked as the Japanese woman moved on.

"We're loggers," Jack said.

"Loggers?"

"The oil rig sort," Steve explained. "I'm a defrocked geologist, and Jack here is half an engineer. Two fine gentlemen gone to seed, between jobs, en route from Albufeira to Caracas."

The plane jumped, a chorus of creaks and jingles. "Riding the cheapest tickets," Jack added.

"Half an engineer?"

Jack shrugged. "Never finished my degree. The 2009 crisis and all that."

She looked at Steve, who was theatrically mouthing *lazy*.

"And what do you exactly mean with 'defrocked'?"

"He killed his research coordinator," Jack said.

"I should have," Steve said. He coughed in mock embarrassment. "Let's say I was not exactly popular with the research funding committee."

"Too much math and not enough rocks," Jack said.

The plane shook again, big drops of water splashing against the windows.

The voice of the captain came through the loudspeakers. In the garbled hubbub, "turbulence" and "rough" were the only words Sandra could understand.

"Here goes," Jack said, looking grimly out of his window. He caught the eye of the girl sitting in front of him, and quickly folded the table in its compartment. "Let's see what happens."

The girl looked at him like he was some kind of freak.

"It will be all right," Steve said with a smile. He tried to fold the table, but the thing was stuck. Sandra tried to lend a hand, but soon they had to admit their defeat.

"Won't be this that kills us," Steve said. He closed his eyes and started breathing deeply again.

Sandra leaned back in her seat, distractedly checking her seat belt buckle. More drops splashed on the glass.

#

Hernan Barreto was thinking about what waited in Caracas, rehearsing his lines in his mind for the hundredth time. The Japanese woman materialized out of thin air by his seat. One of those that Nakasone had left behind, he reasoned. A Peruvian Nisei. They had been often in the news, in the '90s, when he was a kid. Their families had moved to Peru in the 1970s. They had helped establish a Japanese foothold in the South American economy, but when the bubble burst, they found out that Japan was not willing to welcome them back. They were left to their own devices, often described as an embarrassment by the Japanese right-wingers. They had failed. Then they plain disappeared from the news and from everybody's memory. Or at least from Hernan's. Not that he had cared much about them back then: he had been in high school and found the whole story pretty funny. *L'Apocalipse de los Chinos.*

He turned and looked at his Maria sitting across the aisle, listening to David Guetta on her iPhone. Her face was curtained by a wave of her curly black hair, and he could only see the tip of her chin, the curve of her breasts wrapped in the fine linen of her simple white dress. The silver cross hung in her cleavage. What a beautiful thing she was.

"Yes?" he said, turning to the Nisei woman.

"We are going through a pocket of bad weather," she said in a level voice. "Please fasten your seatbelts."

Hernan gave her his best smile and fumbled with the safety buckle.
"Are we expecting trouble?" he asked. "Delays?"

She smiled reassuringly. "We are not anticipating any delay."

"Fine, this is good because I am expected in Caracas and..."

She nodded. "There will be no delays," she said again. Then she turned, slowly walking back to the front of the plane.

Damn. He was so nervous, so charged for what was waiting in Caracas, he thought he would burst if he did not tell somebody. Only he could not tell anybody. Not really.

Hernan stretched a hand out and touched his Maria's hand. She turned and smiled at him, lost in her music. He smiled back, and gestured for her to strap herself in. He looked as she pulled the belt tight around her slender waist, her head bobbing slightly to the rhythm in her ears. The heavy silver cross hanging from her neck danced as she moved, sparkling in the artificial lights. It felt good, knowing that she was his. Walking in the meeting with his wife on his arm would signal to the Venezuelan buyers he was no small fry. A proper exec, not just his father's gopher.

It would be good. Everything would be good.

The plane jumped, like a car hitting a bump in the road. Then it banked suddenly, and the Nisei woman staggered and fell on one of the front couches. There was loud, rough laughter, and one of the kids sitting there shouted, "Wow, man, what a handful!"

The Nisei woman wrangled free, stood with a curse, and hastened back to the flight cabin. The kid massaged his chest where she had elbowed him, and then laughed out loud. "I think she likes me!"

CHAPTER 2

"What the hell is happening?" Rosita hissed, sliding back in her post. She cursed. The windshield was flooded, visibility down to nothing.

"The monster got us," Mike replied. He now looked less like a stray cat and more like a very scared raccoon. Rosita flipped the wipers on, but it did not help much.

Mike banked again, using the wind to clean the view. The air pressure pushed the water away, and they could see the churning blackness beyond. She wondered if it was one of the things he had learned when he was flying fighters, that banking thing. Then he started a steady rise, trying to keep the plane under control. Outside the sky was a solid black mass, like the dead of night. Mike looked more focused than before, more reactive. Like he was actually surfing on trouble.

Rosita put on the headphones. The radio gave her only static. "Freak storm," she said. She needed to talk, simply because the hollow rumble of the storm was getting on her nerves. Mike grunted.

The altimeter climbed slowly. The wind strength increased; the airspeed indicator got wild. The stall alarm started buzzing. For a long moment they were perfectly still, frozen in mid-air in the middle of the maelstrom. Rosita felt a chill, felt butterflies in her belly. Then the Pilatus nose-dived towards the jungle below. Somebody shouted in the back, sudden exclamations of fear mixed with the cheerful voices of the two American kids.

Mike cursed and maintained his hold over the controls. He seconded the diving curve, letting the plane find its natural balance. He touched the controls gently and took the plane out of a slow, ample spiral. With the nose pointed again to the black sky, the engine roared its frustration.

A shape, blacker than black, zipped past on their left, the landscape monochrome in the light of a thunderbolt.

"What was that?"

"Rocks."

"What?!"

Squinting into the night-black outside, Rosita started reciting the standard mayday signal. "This is Sligo Air 001, en route from Albufeira to Caracas. Our current position is..." she glanced at the GPS unit. "Four fourteen north, sixty-five thirty-eight west. Repeat..."

The radio hissed in her ears. "I only get static."

"Keep trying."

The engine hiccupped. Mike cursed. "Should have listened to you and set down at Tama-Tama."

"Big consolation now, thanks a lot, Mike."

She repeated her call for help, again receiving only the buzz of nothingness in response.

"The altimeter's gone," Mike said matter-of-factly.

"Gone? Whaddyamean gone?"

The instrument's hands were twirling madly.

"Look left, girl!"

She turned and stared at a solid wall of nothing. She was about to say something when a lightning flash illuminated the sheer side of a rock face, running headlong by their side, maybe two hundred yards away. In the stark, black and white burst of the lightning, she saw a mighty waterfall tumbling down the side of the cliff. She screeched a curse as Mike banked away from the mountain.

The plane kept rising in the pouring rain, staying away from the crest of the mountains to the northeast. The wind gripped it and it rolled to the south, the engine sputtering, all the alarms flashing and chiming. Then the full power of lightning hit the metal body of the plane, the instruments panel erupting in a cloud of sparks.

In the orange light of the fire coming from the engine's hood, Rosita mechanically extracted the fire extinguisher and put out the flames leaking from the instruments panel. The acrid smell of burnt plastic choked her as she tried the radio again. By her side, Mike kept fighting the lost battle against the storm. The engine coughed and died. The Pilatus was now in the grip of the elements, and wherever they were taking it, there was very little choice for the pilots to make.

#

Dylan and George were howling and waving their arms in the air like they were riding a roller-coaster, and greeted every new crack of thunder with a cheer. Terri hated when they did that. She tried to push up the volume in her earphones, her thumb sliding nervously on the touch screen, killing more colored blocks out of frustration. She cast a passing glance at the thin, bald man sitting in front of her. He was holding a book in his lap. He smiled at her. She turned morosely to the window, staring blankly into the darkness outside.

The idea of an exotic adventure in South America had been so exciting, so romantic. She had imagined herself and Dylan as they explored Machu Picchu and the Mayan cities of Yucatan as they followed the Amazon in a canoe. Alone, in the last uncontaminated place on Earth. It would have been like a movie.

The plane jerked and rolled on the side, and for a moment she caught a glimpse of the dark gray snake of a river as it cut through the almost black expanse of the forest.

It would have been a dream.

And then, that jerk George had shown up at the airport, doing his bro thing and carrying a huge backpack. And Dylan informed her that her boyfriend's beefy college roommate would be joining them.

"Sharing expenses," Dylan had said.

Terri's jaw clenched as frustration simmered inside her.

With George in tow they had been able to book three full weeks, true, but the dream of a romantic adventure had vanished pretty soon. She admitted it had been fun at the start. George was always making stupid jokes and getting in embarrassing situations with the locals. She could laugh at his antics and still hold Dylan's hand, bask in his attention.

Then, Dylan's attitude started getting to her in all the wrong ways. Soon Terri realized he was following George's lead, playing along, imitating his friend's attitude and manners, even his speech patterns. She had said to herself that it was her fault, that she was resenting the fact that she was not the center of Dylan's attention. And she should have been! But the cute, goofy guy she was in love with acted like an idiot, like some stupid frat boy, and was clearly having much more fun with his pal than with his girlfriend.

Things got heavy. The vacation turned into a blur of frustration, misery, and forced fun. Too much booze, too much partying. Weed, too. George seemed capable of scoring some MJ anywhere they went. Terri was no prude, and she liked sharing a joint with her boyfriend. She had long fantasized about getting high on a Mexican beach, under the moon, cradled in the arms of her lover. But her fantasy had not included that jerk George doing a stoned impression of Nicholas Cage, with his shorts on his head, while Dylan laughed his ass off and clapped.

Something caught her attention, and she focused on the window. A huge shape with flapping wings matched speed with the plane.

A condor?

Frowning, she leaned closer to the pane to get a better look. Lightning illuminated a long triangular head, a mouth filled with sharp, triangular teeth.

Then the lights went out. The world exploded.

#

"Do you see that?"

In front of them, the jungle opened in a narrow strip of grassland, running along a pale rocky ridge. It was coming at them at full speed, and already the tallest trees in the jungle, jutting above the canopy, were whizzing by.

"What do you want to do?"

Mike straightened his back.

"I'm taking us down."

Rosita was goggle-eyed. "There?!"

The place was no landing strip. There were trees in the way, and what looked like rock spurs.

"We're gonna die," she whispered.

"It's our only chance. Landing gear?"

She pressed the control. A light blinked and went out. "Dead."

Without waiting for instructions, she bent down and started cranking the manual release. "Okay, it's going."

The landing gear dropped, and the plane felt the change of balance, stalling.

"Hold on tight," he whispered.

The Pilatus descended into the jungle, the long hood wrapped in flames, the engine coughing bursts of black smoke that the beating rain dispersed and washed away. The propeller turned idly. The ground emerged from the darkness, a sudden expanse of trees and branches.

The lightning flashed and for a brief moment Mike was back in Desert Sabre, flying by night and too close to the ground, and the poor losers down there firing their Kalashnikovs at his F15 Eagle. But it was just a moment. No one was firing at the Pilatus.

The left wing cut through the top of a tall tree, and the plane slid and turned, crashing into the vegetation with its side. The right wing bent, snapped and flew off, lost in the dark.

It was at that point that Mike did his magic. *We refuse to die*, they had said in the desert, and here, too, he refused to die, refused to surrender. The plane was his machine; he was in control. He would not die today.

He managed to drag the plane to the grassland at the base of the ridge. The Pilatus touched down, and the landing gear ripped off as the wheels struck a protruding rock. The propeller bent out of shape and finally broke away, twirling like a mad spinning top. The plane cut a swath through the thick, lush undergrowth, animals fleeing in panic in a cacophony of wild calls. It slid and bumped, rotating onto its side before finally coming to rest with a loud crash against a rocky ridge, the chopped-off wing squashed against the stone in a storm of broken glasses and contorted metal.

The tail cone had been ripped off as the plane slammed into a rock spur jutting like a spike from the ground. Suitcases and packs and their contents lay scattered like multi-colored bread crumbs in the mutilated aircraft's wake. Lightning flashed over the scene, casting stark shadows on the wreck's run. The plane cut a swath through the thick, lush undergrowth, animals fleeing in panic in a cacophony of wild calls. It slid and bumped and finally it came to rest with a loud crash against a rocky ridge, the chopped-off wing squashed against the stone in a storm of broken glass and contorted metal.

The beating rain smothered the fire, and a cloud of smoke enveloped the dead aircraft. Again, lightning cut through the sky, illuminating the scene.

The storm raged on.

CHAPTER 3

Steve Tanner coughed and shook his head, trying to clear his vision. Emergency lights bathed him in an underwater bluish light that accentuated his sense of oppression. His breath short, he grimaced as he tried to move, the folding table pressing painfully against his side. His seat had detached from its support and now he was sitting askew, the table pinning him in place.

"Jack," he called. "You out there?"

The French woman lay sprawled on the tabletop, almost in his lap, her blond hair a halo around her head. He moved a strand away delicately, and checked her heartbeat by placing two fingers on her neck. She moaned, and tried to move.

Jack staggered to his feet, running a hand over his forehead. "What the heck?"

Steve took it as a sign that his brother was fine. "Let's try and get out of here," he said.

There was someone moaning somewhere. The dark-skinned beauty that had been sitting behind Jack stood and hit her head on the ceiling. Sandra Barillier grunted and lifted her head. Steve pushed away the table and took a deep breath, feeling pain in his side.

"Just the woman I needed," he said.

She squinted at him. "You hurt?" she asked, going from confused wreck survivor to concerned medical professional in one heartbeat.

Jack was trying to wake up the girl that had been sitting in front of him. He pulled the ear-buds delicately out of her ears. She let out a faint wail. Steve half stood, his head swimming, careful to avoid banging his head somewhere. The air was thick with smoke and the blue emergency light made everything hazy. A flash of white electricity illuminated the cabin, followed by rolling thunder. The back of the cabin was gone. A gaping, ragged hole let in the rain and the night wind. A tangle of vegetation showed as lightning flashed.

"I'm bleeding!" a rough voice screamed in the darkness.

Steve made to move, then simply made way for the doctor as she ran by the side of one of the two kids in the front seats.

The guy's voice became increasingly shrill and panicked. Sandra slapped him in the face. "Hold on!" she said, her voice level. "A broken nose never killed anybody."

The kid looked at her, his face glistening with tears and blood. He kept mumbling, his pal in the silly T-shirt hovering.

The Japanese woman peeped in from the cockpit. She too was bleeding from a number of small cuts on her face. Behind her, the captain was holding her by the shoulders, but whether he was steadying her or using her for support Steve was not able to tell.

"Somebody help me!"

Steve and Jack joined the dark-skinned woman in the white dress as she tried to shake her companion awake. The doctor's couch had detached itself from its swivel base, too, and had trapped a young man. One arm and one shoulder were crushed under the chair.

"Easy, miss," Jack said. "If he's got something broken, you ain't helping him."

She stared at him and nodded. "I'm sorry," she said.

Jack chuckled. "Take it easy." He turned to Steve. "Gimme a hand with the belt. And the chair."

They freed the unconscious man from his safety belt, and then lifted the seat. His left arm was bent at a wrong angle, and he was out for the count.

The hatch opened with a crash, letting in more wind and rain. "Let's get out of here and try to make a point," the captain drawled, walking down the aisle.

#

They filed out of the wreck, the Tanners carrying the unconscious Barreto, his wife walking by their side, limping on a broken three-inch heel. Then Mike and Rosita, then the blond girl, Terri. Sandra closed the line, bleeding George stumbling on, his pal Dylan helping him along. They stood outside, in the light rain. Some stood, some sat down on the soft ground. They looked at the sky as it cleared up in the east, the storm speeding over them on its way to the far mountains.

Past the narrow grassland, trees extended in every direction as far as the eye could see. The airplane had cut a wide track of destruction through the vegetation and the tall grass, leaving long brown scars of exposed soil. Unknown animals called in the jungle. The smell of burnt plastic and gasoline was so thick the rain could not wash it away.

But the rain did wake Hernan Barreto up. He thrashed and jerked and squealed until the Tanners put him down. Then he embraced his wife, one arm around her shoulders, one arm hanging limp at his side.

Sandra pushed a hand into her pocket and came out with a big satellite phone. She adjusted the short, fat antenna, and pressed a few buttons. The thing lit up and she waited, and then she shook her head. No signal. Jack Tanner and Maria Barreto both checked their phones and drew a blank.

Everybody turned to Mike O'Reilly, where he stood shifting his weight from one foot to another.

"Okay," Mike said, clearing his throat. "It's been a rough one, but I guess we can count ourselves lucky. Is everybody fine?"

There was a moment of silence.

"Everybody fine?" the blond girl, Terri, said through clenched teeth. The rain plastered her hair to her cheeks, making her look like a screeching banshee. "Is everybody fine?!"

She started laughing. "You sick old fuck, you almost killed each and every one of us, and you have the gall to ask us if we are fine? Well, no, I'm not fine! I'm soaking wet, scared, bruised, lost in the middle of nowhere with you asking me if I'm fine. How the fuck could I be fine?"

Laughter shook her thin frame and soon turned into deep, dry sobs. She crouched down, sitting on her heels. Her boyfriend, Dylan, looked at her like it was the first time he ever saw her. Sandra moved close to the girl and tried to soothe her, but Terri just pushed her away.

Mike took a deep breath.

"We were hit by lightning," he said. "We can count ourselves lucky for being here, and all of us in one piece."

George pressed a piece of gauze to his nose and mumbled something.

"Yeah," Dylan spat. "Quite some luck."

"Now the draft has cleared the air somewhat, I think we should get back in, and wait for the light of day," Mike said. "Rescue will be on its way in a few hours, we just have to hold on."

"At least we'll be dry," Jack Tanner said. He looked up at the sky. "Dry-ish."

#

"Where are we exactly?" Barreto asked as his wife helped him sit on one of the couches. The doctor knelt by his side and started examining his arm.

Mike turned to Rosita. "Somewhere north and east of the Venezuelan-Brazilian Border," she said. "The Canaima area, if you are familiar with the local geography."

Steve Tanner huffed, shaking his head. "The Bermuda Triangle of South America," he said, pushing wet hair out of his eyes.

"What do you mean?" Barreto's wife asked.

Steve shrugged. "This is the same stretch of nothing where Leonard Clark disappeared back in—it was 1957, I think. Thick, unexplored jungle in every direction, with mountains thrown in for good measure. Weird chap, Clark—"

"And Colonel Fawcett, too," Jack added.

"No," Steve said. "Fawcett disappeared way south, almost on the Argentina border."

Everybody was staring at them.

"But this is no longer 1957," Mike said defensively.

"Which is good," Steve Tanner replied, smiling.

Barreto screamed, cursed, then shut his eyes, his face flustered.

"The radius and the cubitus are broken," Sandra Barillier said. "Moving him was not a good idea."

"We couldn't leave him stretched beneath a stuffed chair, doc, breathing dioxin." Jack Tanner smiled.

"You could have waited for me," she replied, piqued. "Now we need to set the fracture and then splint it."

"We?"

"There's a first aid kit behind my seat," Mike said, but Rosita was already moving.

"What about the ELT?" Jack Tanner asked.

"What about it?" Mike asked back.

The two men stared at each other, and then Tanner shook his head. "Nothing, I was being stupid."

Mike nodded. "The ELT is working fine," he said. "It was built to withstand every sort of punishment."

The emergency locator transmitter was in the tail cone of the plane, and right now the tail cone of the plane was somewhere out there, in the trees, under the rain. Half a mile away, maybe more. It was not a big deal. The thing had been designed to survive exactly this kind of accident, and it was certainly working, broadcasting its distress call. But discussing its current position would have only caused more worries in the passengers. Mike appreciated Tanner's discretion.

#

The doctor opened the kit.

"I have much better tools, but they are stocked in the hold," she said.

"And the hold is probably two miles from here," Jack Tanner replied.

Sandra snorted, handed him the bag to hold, and started working. Rosita hovered by, holding a big field light. The doctor mumbled a thank you and gestured for her to move closer.

Barreto squealed some more, his wife holding his good hand. "The analgesics will kick in in a moment," Sandra said. She stood and looked around. "Anyone else in need of medical assistance?" She faced the older Tanner. "What about your ribs?"

"I'll live." Steve grinned.

"If you don't mind, I'd like to be the one to say that."

With a smirk, he lifted his fishing vest and his shirt, exposing a large bruise stretching across his side. She bent and prodded the bruise gently. "Hurts?"

"Only when I laugh."

She gave him a long stare. "The ribs seem all right. Have trouble breathing?"

He took a deep breath, in and out. "No."

She nodded.

"Will I live?" he asked cheerfully.

"You'll live," she said, serious.

"Think about the girl," he said in a whisper.

Sandra nodded.

She went to the girl's chair and knelt down by her side.

"Are you hurt?" she asked. The girl shrugged.

"I can give you a mild sedative, if you want. I won't recommend it, but if you feel you need it..."

"I need to be alone," Terri replied.

Sandra stared into her face, trying to see what was going on there. Then she stood and shot a deadly glance at Dylan and George, who had been leering at her bum while she talked with Terri. The kids laughed. She wondered passingly if they were stoned.

CHAPTER 4

The following morning, mist rising in the early rays of the sun, the main cabin was humid and stale, and spirits were highly flammable.

"Stop whining!" Mike blurted out. Hernan Barreto had been complaining again, and Mike could not stand to have the same damn conversation all over again.

"There is a flight plan," he said. "There's a GPS track, there's an automatic distress signal. We did send a distress call before our landing..."

"Great landing, by the way." The Big Bang Theory kid smirked. Mike heard him and turned.

"Maybe you'll do better the next time, kid," he said, pointing his finger at him.

The boy lifted his arms, as if in surrender. "Cool it, man!"

"Cool my ass!"

Mike knew that the hostility was a sign that the pressure was getting to them, and he knew it was all right if they hit upon him. But he was not going to be their punching ball. He turned back to Barreto. "This is the twenty-first century," he said, regaining some of his control. "This is no Lost. This is not," he waved a hand at Steve, "the Bermuda Triangle of Whatever. You just can't disappear like that anymore. We've got GPS, sat imagery, the works. They know we didn't land as scheduled, and they are probably already looking for us. In a few days they'll come and get us."

"Who?" Barreto asked. "Who's looking for us?"

Mike shrugged. "It's not like I'm asking them out to dance, mister. The Venezuelan air force, most likely. Or the Brazilians. Or Jungle Girl. I'm not asking them for their pedigree when they come with their Range Rovers and their choppers to take us home, as long as they come fast."

He looked around. Everybody was pacified, or at least resigned.

"How fast?" the blond girl asked.

"What?"

"How long will they take? To come here and rescue us?"

Mike ran a hand through his crew-cut. "Hard to say. They'll send out search aircraft first. So we'll need to do our best to get spotted. But that will be easy. We are in plain sight, no tree cover. As soon as they spot us, they'll get moving. Protocols will kick in, men will be deployed. So, to answer your question, miss, anywhere between two days and a week."

"A week?!" Barreto exclaimed. His wife put a hand on his arm and whispered something. He shook her off and took a step forward. "This is absolutely unacceptable."

Mike pushed his hands in his pockets. "Sorry to disappoint you, mister, but as you can see, everybody's plans went somewhat awry after last night."

#

"We could try and salvage the radio," Jack Tanner said. "While we are waiting, I mean."

"You know how to do it?" Rosita said.

The younger of the Tanner boys shrugged and patted his side, pulling a Leatherman tool from a belt pouch. "Might give it a try."

"We should have some better tools than that," she said.

"I'll work with Mister Tanner here," Mike said. He grunted, working out the kinks in his neck by moving his head from one side to the other. "I'd kill for some coffee."

Steve Tanner rummaged in one of his vest pockets and offered him a chocolate bar. "We'll need to find water, and take stock of our supplies."

"You guys said that help was on the way," Dylan said. "Got more chocolate, man?"

"As our captain pointed out," Steve handed him a bar, "they'll need time."

Mike grunted, chewing on his breakfast chocolate. "There's a lot of small airports in the area," he said. "If they got our SOS, there will be search flights, and it's not like they can ignore the mess we made landing."

"If they got the SOS?"

Rosita closed her eyes and took a deep breath. *Please not again.* "Mister Barreto, it's not like we were in optimal conditions."

"And what if they did not catch our SOS?" Barreto asked.

Mike shook his head, sighing, but it was Rosita that replied. "We should have been in Caracas twelve hours ago," she said. "So they know that something happened to us. What will happen is this." She started counting on her fingers. "The Caracas airport authorities will send out a query, checking with all the airports in the area to see if we landed there. Tama-Tama, Santa Barbara del Amazonas, Manapiare, El Yavi, Auaris, Surucucu. Fonte Boa too."

She arched her eyebrows and checked her watch. "This already happened, by the way. Having received a negative check, the air traffic authorities will know that we got in trouble after our fueling stop in Fonte Boa. They'll raise the alarm—"

"And the news will start broadcasting about the missing plane," Steve Tanner said.

Rosita glanced at him. "That too, yes. Our consulates will make inquiries, journalists will drive to our relatives' homes to interview our spinster aunt, take a photo of the cat, check out our school records, the works. At this point, the air forces in Venezuela and Brazil will have the ball, and they will coordinate and start their search flights. They will spot us—"

"You sound pretty sure they will."

"Oh, they will. There's nothing but airports hereabouts, which is good, because it means that search flights will cover a lot of area in very little time. They will spot us all right, a white and silver wreck against the dark green of the grass and the forest."

"And we will see them," Mike said, "and we'll fire a few flares."

"And they will send along a rescue team," Rosita concluded. "Army, probably."

Barreto dragged himself to one of the seats. "How long will it take?"

Yawning, his wife sat by his side, and laid her head on his shoulder.

"As the captain said, that depends on a lot of things—weather, cloudy cover, search pattern," Rosita said. "Could take anything from twelve hours to a week."

"Shit, man!" George said.

"And that's why we need to find water and food," Steve said.

"Exactly," Mike said. He waited as Doctor Barillier and Dylan's girlfriend joined them.

"I'll check the radio with Mister Tanner," he said then. "And I guess we'll need the doctor here to look after Mister Barreto's arm."

"There should not be any complication," Sandra said. "But I'll also take an inventory of what supplies we have here."

"And that will be a short job," George said, grinning, "because we lost most of our luggage." He leered at Rosita. "Some monkey will be trying on your lingerie."

The woman stared at him. "Maybe they are sticking with yours. Monkeys like pink and frilly."

"Bang!" Dylan laughed. "Owned, man!"

Neither George nor Terri were smiling.

Mike looked at the three kids. "Right, so you guys could go and retrieve our lost luggage."

George gave a long look at the jungle surrounding them, then stared back at Mike. "Who decided you are the one giving orders, old man?"

"He is the captain," Jack Tanner said, his voice low.

"And a fine job he did!"

"You got a better idea?" Rosita asked him. "Or any skill we could use here at base camp?"

George shrugged, pushing his hands in his pockets.

"I guessed so," she sneered. She turned to Steve Tanner. "You a rock hound, right? You know where to look for water?"

"Yes, and yes. Let's say I can work that out."

"Fine, then we'll go and look for water, and do a bit of exploring." She gave George a hard stare. "I need a change of air."

The young man made a face and flipped her the bird, but only after she had turned her back to him.

#

"I need to keep repeating to myself that I can do this," Rosita said, slapping her neck. Her fingers were sticky with sweat. She had tied her black hair in a ponytail, but this seemed only to make the mosquitoes' life easier.

Steve Tanner nodded and stopped to wait for her. She was actually a lot fitter than him, and about ten years his junior, but she kept stopping for breath, and he did not dare tell her that she should talk less and save her breath and moisture. She was somewhat intimidating, despite her small size.

They had been following what they had been calling "a track," but that still felt like thick, unadulterated undergrowth trying to rip her clothes off and inflict on her a selection of small cuts, scratches and bruises.

"Fucking jungle!" she grumbled.

There were fallen trees that had been rotting for ages. Bushes and clumps of ferns. And clear tracts too, where the ground was like a felt carpet, or covered with a layer of pine needles.

"And weird, too," Steve replied.

"Weird how?"

Steve pursed his lips. "I don't know, I'm no botanist. But there's a lot of unusual plants hereabouts. Like," he pointed at a thicket of trees, "I never saw palms and conifers mix. And ferns. You don't usually think of ferns when you think about the Amazon basin. Or do you?"

She held his stare. "I'm no botanist either," she said flatly.

"Yes, of course. And these plateaus are famous for their unusual and unique ecosystems—"

Rosita crossed her arms. "You are not playing a part, are you?"

"What do you mean?"

Distractedly, she slapped her arm. "You really like this stuff. The plants and plateaus and whatever—"

He grinned back. "Talking too much, am I?"

Rosita looked around. She had no idea if the trees were weird or if there were too many ferns or too few aspidistras. "Let's say I'd be concerned with more immediate matters, such as, you sure we can find water in this direction?"

He nodded. "The subsoil is sandstone and limestone. We are walking downhill and following a track. Most likely it will lead us to some watering hole."

She nodded, drying sweat from her forehead with her sleeve. "Lead on," she sighed.

"You should have stayed back with my brother," he said over his shoulder. "Try and fix the radio."

She snorted. "I needed—"

"What?"

She shushed him. "Listen."

There was a distant sound, like a low buzzing.

"A plane," she said.

They both looked up. The jungle canopy was too thick for them to see anything. Shadows scuttled along the branches, chirping in fear. "Turboprop," Rosita said. She checked her watch. "Out of Manapiare, probably. Or El Yavi."

"Good news?"

She shrugged. "The sun is in a good position for sighting the wreck. So yes, it is good news."

Tanner gave a deep sigh. "Fine."

She gave him a smile. "Feeling better?"

"Aren't you?"

Rosita chuckled. "Yeah. But you know, I keep bitching to give myself something to do. You and your brother made a nice work showing a brave face."

He shook his head. "It's not that. It's just that giving in is useless. We don't sit and despair. We'd rather do something."

"You and your brother have been around, I guess."

"You could say that, yes."

She took a deep breath, and again ran a hand over her sweaty neck. She made a face. "Well, you'll have to tell me how you ended up on our flight. But we still have to find water for Señora Barreto's drinks."

Steve laughed, and Rosita found herself laughing too. "Bitching, right?"

"She's all right, I guess," he said.

"Oh, she's pretty hot," she corrected him. "And the two frat boys are stripping her with their eyes."

"You shouldn't be jealous." He grinned, pushing a clump of low branches out of the way, and nodding for her to pass. "She's not the only one they are stripping with their eyes."

Rosita took the lead, giving him a sideways glance.

"Aren't you a smooth one," she quipped. Then she chuckled. "But yeah, you're probably right. Broken Nose even made a grab for me yesterday."

"You kidding?"

"No sir. He felt my ass, the slimy bastard." She gave a sigh. "Kids. It's part of their role, right? I guess he thought he was paying me a compliment."

"Probably."

They were on the lip of a gentle slope, the trees giving way to short grasses over rocky ground, boulders emerging here and there like sea rocks along a beach. They marched slowly eastwards, side by side. "But I'd be careful, when it comes to Maria Barreto," she said, winking.

They started marching slowly eastwards, side by side. He stopped. "What do you mean?"

"That Mister Barreto looks to me like the sort of guy that can be really dangerous if he feels his property is being tampered with. You heard how he got all worked up about his engagements in Caracas and his frigging Louis Vuitton suitcases."

"I can assure you that my intentions towards Miss Barreto are completely honorable." Steve grinned.

"Yeah, sure."

She looked around. The ground was level in all directions, the jungle thick with humidity, shrubs and ferns growing at the base of the trees. "Which way now?"

He checked his compass, then pocketed it. "That way," he pointed.

"And don't even get me started about that poor silly girl, Big Bang's girlfriend," she said. She put her hands on her hips and drew a deep sigh. "Yeah, I know, I'm bitching."

Tanner laughed, and picked his way through the vegetation.

#

"The old guy is really just a prick," George said. "But the little geisha is quite a piece of ass."

23

Terri glanced at him.

They were following the path the plane had carved into the vegetation, looking for the lost luggage. Sandra Barillier had made it very clear that the top priority was finding the emergency pack and her red suitcase, which contained medical supplies and equipment.

But the guys had other priorities.

"Man, the idea of a dark blue backpack was not cool at all," Dylan said.

"You didn't want to carry Mary Jane in your red fancy pack," George replied. He kicked a broken branch and pushed his hands deep into the pockets of his shorts.

They had been carrying a big bag of weed that the boys had bought in Albufeira. Terri snorted. "Can't you think about anything else?"

George gave her a look. "You seemed to like it, back in Whatsitsname."

He put his thumb and forefinger to his lips and pretended to suck on a joint. Coming up behind her, Dylan encircled her waist with his arms and pushed his head against her shoulders, kissing her neck. "And I do think about something else, babe," he said.

"Oh, c'mon, you two, get a room!"

Terri shrugged Dylan off with an irritated hiss.

"We're in the middle of a fucking jungle!"

"Well, in Albufeira we were on a park bench," Dylan jeered.

"Exactamundo," George said, jumping up onto a chunk of rock. "And you were totally stoned, and a lot of fun. So, case closed."

He scanned the horizon. The plane had plowed a two-hundred-yard corridor in the vegetation before it reached the grassland, chopping small trees and digging into the ground.

"There it is!"

George pointed. Out in the distance, they could make out the outline of the plane's tail cone, resting upended among the foliage.

"Which means the bags should be hereabouts," Dylan said.

"Shut up!"

"You shut up!"

Terri shook her head. "No, listen! Can you hear it?"

They could.

"It's a plane!" George shouted, jumping off his perch.

They scanned the sky. "The old man was right. They are looking for us!"

Suddenly, the black silhouette of a plane entered their field of vision. It was flying low and slow.

They started shouting and waving their arms, jumping up and down.

George took his football jersey off and started waving it like a flag, red against the brown and green of the jungle.

The plane flew over them, and then, its engines changing tone, took a slow turn and flew over them again. They cheered and shouted and waved, more than before. Then, a red light appeared in the sky, a flare shot from their grounded plane, hovering there for a while and then slowly hovering down to the ground, impossible to miss. The plane did a third passage, tipping its wings, and then flew back in the direction from which it had come.

"C'mon, hon," George said. "Take it off and flash them your tits! They'll come and rescue us faster."

She told him to fuck off.

"I really prefer you when you are stoned, you know." He grinned, putting his jersey back on.

"Which means," Dylan said, "that we must absolutely find Mary Jane!" They laughed. "But now we better get back to the plane and see what our fearless commander wants us to do."

"Righto!" George said. "And if he really is in a hurry, he can come and pick up his valise himself."

Terri looked up at the sky again, wondering how long the rescuers would take.

#

Mike put down his flare gun.

"They saw it," he said.

Jack patted his shoulder. "Now we just need to wait."

Mike nodded.

There were a lot of things running in his mind right then—inquiries, safety commissions, insurance revisions and all the rest. He had lost his plane, and his license was probably on the line right now.

But right now, it was okay. Help was on the way.

Jack returned to the cockpit for a final attempt at reviving the damaged radio.

"It doesn't matter if the radio's fried," Mike said, following him. "Now we just have to stay put, and wait for the bus to stop and bring us back home."

CHAPTER 5

"Well, this sort of changes things, I guess."

Rosita cursed and sat down heavily, her arms hanging between her crossed legs.

They were on the brink of a cliff, white rock dropping vertically for about two hundred feet. At the foot of the escarpment, hazy for the mist, the jungle stretched for about two miles towards the east, and then gave way to a vast, monotonous, white-blue sea of clouds. North and south, the cliff stretched like a vertical wall for two or three miles in both directions, until it faded into the cloudy cover. Other plateaus loomed in the distance, like stone rafts adrift on a cotton-candy ocean, each one topped by a thin layer of greenery.

"We are on top of a frigging mesa," Rosita said. "One of those places. What they call them? A tespool."

"*Tepui*," Tanner corrected her. "It's a local word that means house of the gods."

"Shit!"

With her heel, she kicked a loose stone and watched it fall, as if in slow motion, until it disappeared through the dense network of branches down there. A flock of tiny birds scattered below, screeching.

"It's not like we can just walk away from here," she said. "And it means they'll have to send choppers to get us."

"As far as I know, only three of the Gran Sabana's tepuis can be reached by foot," Tanner said.

"Shit!" she repeated.

"You have quite a potty mouth, you know?"

"Fuck off."

Steve crouched down beside her. "Let's look on the bright side of things," he said kindly.

She gave him a look. He pointed to their right. About half a mile to the south, a waterfall poured from the upper plateau, an arch of sparkling water wreathed in a rainbow cloud.

"We found water," he said.

She chuckled bitterly. "Yeah, so now we can drown ourselves."

#

They walked down a barren escarpment to the place where the

stream cut into the lip of rock and fell down the cliff. The water had cut a narrow corridor in the basement rock and formed a sort of bowl where the path crossed the stream. The trees drooped over the stream, and the air was heavy with humidity and the smell of wet dirt.

"There's a lake down there," Steve said.

"Really?" Rosita splashed in the stream, water coming to her ankles.

"The rock's limestone. The waterfall must have eroded a small basin down there."

"Fine. And can we drink it?"

Steve shrugged. "My grandfather taught me that if there's mosquito larvae in it, it's good to drink."

She gave him a look. She slapped a hand on her neck, killing a mosquito. "Your grandfather? Aren't you supposed to be a geologist or something?"

He shrugged. "Miss, I just found you the stream you needed," he said. "Now you'll need a biologist to tell you if the water's good. Or a chemist. Or both. It's called big science. We geologists don't do it."

He pulled a plastic cup from his backpack and filled it. "Or you'll have to rely on somebody to drink it."

He took a long gulp of water and sighed happily.

"Cold, sweet, and perfectly safe in the short term. Maybe a bit hard, but that's to be expected. Limestone, you know—"

She grinned and took the cup from his hand. "We have no time for the long term," she said and drank in turn.

He took off his pack, sat on a rock and pulled out two folding tanks.

"What's the hurry?" she asked. "We should still have plenty of light, right?" They had moved through the twilight of the jungle for so long, she had lost the sense of time. She bent down and filled her cup again. "Now we'll have to find some food, but things look up, I guess. Help is on its way."

"I'd rather not spend too much time in this place," he said.

Rosita sipped her water. "Why?"

Tanner looked around. "Animals. Coming here to drink." He pointed at a tree. "See that?"

Rosita squinted. About two feet from the ground, the bark had been stripped off the bole, exposing the pale wood underneath for a good three feet.

"I'd rather steer clear of the beast that rubs itself against that tree when it comes here to drink."

"Shouldn't they come only at sunset and dawn?" she asked.

"You were in Girl Scouts?"

She cursed under her breath and picked up one of the tanks.

"Let's fill these and get back," she said.

Steve Tanner just nodded and kept staring at the ground, looking for traces of other animals.

#

"So, people," Mike said, "looks like the good news is, we've been spotted, and help is on its way."

"And the bad news?" Hernan Barreto asked. They were gathered outside of the wreck of the Pilatus.

"The bad news is, we are on a very high plateau. A tepui."

The others exchanged glances.

"Which means?" Maria Barreto asked.

Steve cleared his voice. "Tepuis are the remains of a large sandstone plateau that once covered the granite basement complex between the north border of the Amazon Basin and the Orinoco, between the Atlantic coast and the Rio Negro, during the Precambrian period."

His brother just chuckled and shook his head.

"Over millions of years," Steve went on, "the plateaus were eroded and all that was left were isolated, flat-headed tepuis. The name means house of the gods, incidentally. Imagine a box-like mountain, with a flat top, anywhere from one thousand to three thousand meters high. That's where we are, on top of one of those. This one seems to be chiefly composed of sandstone, with limestone layers." He looked around. "Not that anybody cares about that, I guess."

Barreto was aghast. "You gotta be kidding!"

"Like the Roraima," Terri said.

Steve looked at her, smiling. "Exactly."

"We wanted to go there," she said in a small voice, glancing at Dylan. "They do backpacking tours of the summit. But then we canceled that..."

"Well, see?" George grinned, hugging her, ignoring how stiff she was. "You got your dream vacation anyway. And we'll also get a refund and damage compensation."

"Will this make things more complicated?" Maria asked. "I mean, they spotted us, so...?"

"They will have to send helicopters, but that was an option from the beginning," Mike explained. "Now it all depends from where the choppers will have to come from. It might take a day or two more than we expected."

Barreto snorted. "And in the meantime, what do we do?"

"We could start a fire," Jack said. "It would keep us warm, keep the wild animals away, and signal our position."

"And it would make our meager dinner cozier, if not tastier," Steve added. "Then, tomorrow, we'll go back and recover the luggage."

He stared at George.

"Hey, man, I mean, there was a plane in the sky, right? We thought we needed to get back and plan stuff, see? Like we did. Be cool, we'll go and find your suitcase tomorrow morning. But we saw the plane and we decided it was better to drop everything and get back."

The group dispersed.

Steve and Rosita traded a glance. "Lazy motherfucker," Rosita said.

"Yeah, never seen someone so excited for a plane since the short guy in Fantasy Island."

Rosita laughed.

#

The Tanners set to work on building a fire for the night.

Jack started digging a pit using a scrap of metal. "To contain the fire," he said. In the meantime, his brother set out to collect wood.

"This stuff is so wet," Steve said, dropping the first armful of faggots, "that we'll end up smoked like as many salmons."

"Or we could build a sauna." His brother nodded.

They kept working while the rest of the passengers watched.

Rosita sat down on a flat rock, her elbows on her knees.

"I wonder where they find the energy," Sandra said, sitting down by her side.

The Japanese girl glanced at her. "Steve said it's their way of keeping desperation at bay."

"They are good guys."

"Yeah."

Sandra pulled out a pack of Camels and offered her one. Rosita shook her head. "Doctors shouldn't smoke," she said.

Sandra shrugged and lit up. "Father was a doctor. Mother was a doctor. Both my grandparents were doctors. All smokers. All of them lived to a happy old age." She placed the packet on the rock between them. "My ex-husband was a doctor and he didn't smoke. Does it bother you?"

"Got nothing against ex-husbands. Nor doctors."

They laughed.

Jack straightened his back and looked at them, grinning. Rosita waved her hand, then turned to stare self-consciously at Sandra.

"We should find something to do, too," Sandra said. "Things have been frantic and weird. But we must keep ourselves occupied."

"We could build a shower."

They turned. Maria Barreto was standing there. Sandra noticed that even against the background of a wrecked airplane, the young woman was striking a studied pose, and her disheveled hair looked gorgeous anyway, just as her dirty white shift looked fresh off a catwalk.

"Can I bum a smoke?"

Sandra handed her the packet and lighter. "As long as they last."

Maria lit a cigarette. "Hernan hates me smoking," she confessed, taking a long pull.

Rosita shifted and made some room for her to sit down.

"How's your husband's arm?" Sandra asked.

"Fine, for what I can tell. He complains it hurts and," she waved her cigarette in the air, "throbs."

"It's only natural."

They smoked in silence for a while.

"That thing about a shower," Rosita said suddenly.

"Yes?"

"Carrying water is a pain in the ass, but coming back today we spotted a place, along the stream, where there's these," she huffed, "things—Steve gave them a name. Like small pools that the water cut into the rock."

She pointed east. "About two hundred yards in that direction. They look like natural bathtubs."

She looked at the two smoking women. "We could set up a bubble bath expedition." She grinned. "Take Terri along, too."

Maria arched a fine eyebrow. "Wouldn't it be dangerous?"

"The place is reasonably clear, and we could take turns—two take a bath and two keep an eye out."

"And if a wild beast comes," Sandra laughed, "we run naked and covered in suds through the jungle for two hundred yards."

"Or we fight it back using wet towels," Rosita replied with a chuckle. Then she pouted. "It was just an idea."

"We might ask Doctor Tanner," Maria said.

"What?" Rosita glanced at her.

"About the best time to go and have a bath. He seems to know a lot about... stuff." She squashed the spent butt of her cigarette against the rock. "He might have some suggestions."

"He might."

Maria stood and sighed. "Thanks for the smoke," she said. "And for that bubble bath expedition, count me in. I have some Joe Malone in my carry on."

They watched her go back into the wreck.

"Nice girl," Sandra said.

"Yeah, nicer than I thought." Rosita paused for a moment. "Who the hell is Joe Malone?"

"Damned if I know."

The Tanners' bonfire was refusing to light.

Sandra picked up her cigarette packet, opened it, closed it, and put it back. "Better save them for later." She glanced at Rosita.

"What?"

"Nothing."

The bonfire flared with a crackling of sparks. The Tanners applauded and cheered.

"Ladies and gentlemen," Jack announced, "the Crash-land Barbecue and Grill is now open."

CHAPTER 6

"Sir, they have found the plane."

Rainclouds were rolling in over Panama, and from high in the hills the city looked like it was floating over a thin layer of mist. It was almost beautiful.

"Where?"

"In the Amazonas district, sir. They crash-landed in the hills on the border with Bolivar. The Canaima area."

Gabriel Barreto turned from the window. "Are they alive?"

Miguel Fobello took a deep breath. "Probably."

The Old Barreto coughed and squashed his half-smoked cigar in the cut-glass ashtray on the corner of his desk. "Do we know somebody in the right place?" he asked.

Fobello shifted his weight. "We have many contacts in Venezuela," he said. "There is—"

Barreto lifted a hand and shook it, like waving goodbye. The golden ring on his finger sparkled in the dusk of the library. "I don't care who. You call them."

His factotum nodded, his arms stretched down his sides. "Of course. The rescue parties will—"

"No rescue parties," Barreto said.

"Sir?"

The old man sat on his chair and placed his hands on the top of the desk. He fidgeted with his ring, his thumb and forefinger turning it rapidly, like trying to unscrew it from his finger. "We cannot risk somebody finding the files."

"But—"

"No. Get Schneider. We will mount our own rescue party."

"Of course. But the Venezuelans—"

"They will invent an excuse. Bad weather, local tribes, or something."

Fobello bowed. "Of course."

"Go now. Do what needs to be done. And get me Schneider."

The thin man turned and walked to the door. His hand on the handle, he turned.

"Sir."

"What else?"

"I am sure Hernan is fine, sir. And young Miss Barreto, too."

Gabriel snorted. "I don't care," he said, his voice rumbling like distant thunder. "My son has been very stupid, and he will have to face the consequences. We all will have to." He paused, and opened the cigar box. "The rules apply to everybody. No one's exempted. And all those that break the rules have to pay, and pay the same way."

Fobello felt a chill.

"As for his wife," Gabriel went on, rolling a new cigar between his fingers, "she is of no importance." He struck a match. "Go now."

"Yes sir."

Now alone, Gabriel Barreto took a puff from his cigar and closed his eyes. Not for the first time, he wondered where he had gone wrong with the kid.

Hernan had always been a weakling, and he considered the boy's failure his own full responsibility: he had been unable to make a man of his only son. He had tried to give him the best. The schools, first in Switzerland, then in America. The business experience. The travels abroad.

Gabriel had never hidden the unpleasant side of the family trade to his son. The danger, the need to deal with unsavory individuals: politicians, corrupt cops, sometimes even worse specimens of humankind. He had never shielded his son from the truth, and yet Hernan had been unable to make a stepping stone of the experience. He had been unable, or unwilling, to build his own life based on the information.

A weakling and a bully.

They usually turned out that way. Gabriel had been around, had seen them. He despised bullies, especially those that relied on somebody else's strength to back them up. And that, Gabriel knew, was the true heart of the problem: his son did not have the *cojones* to be of any use to the family trade, and yet cherished the privilege and the "face" that being the son of Gabriel Barreto granted. Fast cars, wild parties, big expenses. That trophy wife of his, married in open defiance to Gabriel's instructions.

He had hoped that small, meaningless rebellion would be a first sign of emancipation. He had even hoped this woman might bring out his son's character. But it had just been empty posturing. She was the one with the balls; Hernan was just a puppet.

And now, this hare-brained ploy, these mysterious Venezuelan "friends," and off the kid goes, his wife in tow, she probably the brains of the stupid game. To some meeting or other in Caracas, negotiating God knew what sort of venture behind his father's back. Claiming he was taking a vacation along the coast of Peru. Lying to his own father. And he takes along a copy of the last three years of *everything*. Transactions, payments, deals and agreements, alliances and friendly arrangements. Documents that for some, Gabriel first and foremost, would mean disaster, bankruptcy, scandal. Police investigations. Jail. For eternity.

Information enough to erase three generations of planning and pruning of the network. And Hernan had made a copy, the stupid fool, to show off and impress his prospective buyers. Show them the numbers, tell them where the bodies were, literally, buried. People who could be Interpol, or DEA, or even worse than that.

Gabriel slipped a hand in his pocket, caressing the silver rosary he carried. His mother's rosary. And truly did the Virgin look after her devotees, and now Hernan was marooned somewhere in the jungle.

Possibly wounded. Maybe dead. And with enough information on his body to cost life and freedom for four of the most powerful people in Central America. Including his father. Including Gabriel.

This was not acceptable.

He picked up the phone on the second ring.

"Yes."

"Sir, Major Schneider is on the line for you, sir."

CHAPTER 7

"This place is beautiful!"

And it was.

Where the trees were farther between, the creek had cut through the white rock, creating a slick slide. About halfway along, erosion had excavated two large pools, about ten feet in diameter and five feet deep. Fine white sparkling sand was at the bottom, and the water was perfectly clear.

"It's damn cold!" Rosita said, drying her hand on the leg of her trousers.

"It's just a moment," Terri said, getting rid of her T-shirt. "We bathed in the Humboldt current, in Mexico."

She slipped out of her jeans and dropped her underwear. Then she walked in the creek, sat on the edge of the closest pool, and slipped in. She gasped, jumping from one foot to the other.

"I-i-it's w-wonderf-ful!" she cried through chattering teeth, her eyes wide and sparkling.

The other women laughed.

Sandra nodded at Maria. "In you go. Me and Rosy will take the second turn."

Maria smiled and placed her bundle of towels and fresh clothes by a tree. She undid her chain and placed her silver cross on the folded towels. She shrugged off the white dress. Following Terri's footsteps, she joined her in the water, letting out a shrill gasp.

"One would think her husband could afford to buy her underwear," Rosita whispered through her teeth, turning away.

Sandra chuckled and lit a cigarette.

Maria had brought her Joe Malone Orange Blossom shower oil, and she and Terri flooded the pool with white foam as they massaged their scalp and rinsed their hair. The air was cool and filled with the twittering of invisible birds, and soon it was heavy with the perfume of oranges.

"Would be a nice place for a vacation," Rosita said.

"No thanks," Sandra said, blowing out smoke. "I've spent too much time in forests, jungles, and swamps. My idea of vacation is two weeks in Paris, or London. Shopping."

"I didn't mark you for a Sex and the City sort of girl."

"Who mentioned sex? Public transport, air conditioning, restaurants. Believe me, spend six months in a field hospital, and you'll learn to appreciate even American fast food. There's been nights I'd kill for a Big Mac."

The birds were suddenly silent.

Sandra and Rosita turned to each other. Maria and Terri chattered in their pool. Theirs were the only voices.

Rosita shushed them. "Get out of there!"

"But—"

"No buts, something's wrong."

A low growl echoed through the trees. Maria cursed and hastened out of the water. She slipped on the slick wet stone, and Sandra helped her keep her balance. Rosita scanned the bushes. There was something moving through the undergrowth, slowly circling them. Big, and very quiet. She saw the leaves shaking. Whatever it was, it made a low, liquid purr. Like a big cat.

"A jaguar," she said. Were there jaguars in the Amazon?

"Shouldn't it be afraid of us?" Terri asked.

Maria had slipped into a red dress and held her cross between her lips as she did the clasp of the chain, her things bundled under her arm. Terri jumped on one leg, trying to put on her jeans.

"Probably nobody ever told him he should be afraid."

"Let's get back to the plane," Sandra said. "And quick."

Rosita glanced at the foamy surface of the bathing pool and sighed.

#

"Are you crazy?!"

Hernan Barreto slapped his wife hard, twice, and she took a step back, her eyes burning.

Jack grasped Barreto's good wrist. "Stop it, man!"

"She could have died!" the man exclaimed, tearing away from Jack's hold. "We don't know what sort of beast can be out there! And she goes for a dip in the woods with her girlfriends!"

He turned to Sandra. "Doctor Barillier, I thought you, at least, were a responsible woman, given your age and profession."

Sandra arched an eyebrow.

Rosita saw Steve repress a grin and bit on her tongue not to laugh herself.

"Everything's fine," Mike said, trying to keep the peace. "I was informed of the expedition, an—"

"You were informed?!" Barreto stared at his wife.

Jack was sure that, had he not been between them, Hernan would have hit Maria again.

"You were informed? You? A stranger? And what am I, that my wife risks her life and does not even tell me? What am I?"

"Asleep," she said. Jack turned to stare at her, shivering at the cool spiteful edge on the woman's voice. "You were asleep when we left, and I did not want to wake you up."

Barreto shifted his weight from one foot to the other.

"Well," he said finally, "you should not have been so thoughtful of my rest. Think more of what would have been of me should anything have happened to you."

He shouldered Jack out of the way and embraced his wife.

"You know I couldn't live without you," he whispered.

Holding her tight, he led her inside the plane.

"Now that's the way to treat a woman," Terri said to Dylan.

"Hit her and then say you love her?" Rosita snorted. Terri stared at her.

"Are you sure it was a jaguar?" Jack asked.

Sandra said, "By the noise it made moving through the bushes, it was the size of a big dog. Or a big cat."

The man scratched his beard. "He was probably much more scared of you than you were of him," he said. "But let's keep an eye out from now on. It would be silly to survive a plane crash only to get eaten by a mountain cat."

#

"You don't need to worry, honey," Maria said, running her fingers through Hernan's hair. "Rescue is on its way."

"I hate being unable to move freely," he said, trying to stretch his splinted arm and grimacing.

"Don't worry," she repeated.

He caressed her cheek, and then his hand slid down her neck and fingered the heavy silver cross she wore on a chain. "You could have lost this," he whispered.

She shook her head, snorting softly. "Everything was perfectly under control," she said.

"But you came back running. Not much control, I say."

"I would never lose the key," she said, her hand on his on her chest. "I am not that stupid."

"I know you are not," he said. He took a deep sigh. "What would I do without you?"

She took her hand from his. "You would find another way to move your files," she said.

Hernan snorted. "You are such a cynical bitch. You spoil everything."

"That's why we fit so nicely together, honey," she replied.

He just snorted again.

Maria sat by his side and pulled out her iPod. The silence of the night in this place gave her the creeps. The idea of creatures roaming freely made her more than uneasy. She pumped up the volume, smiled at her husband, and sat in one of the executive chairs. She could see the three kids sitting at the back of the plane, close by the large gash in the fuselage.

They were laughing and talking among themselves. Terri was sitting in Dylan's lap, and he was holding her, an arm around her waist.

Maria smiled and caressed her crucifix. Under her fingertip she felt the hair-thin line of the USB plug cover.

Hernan was brooding.

She sighed. He was like a child. But a child with access to one of the most powerful networks in Central and South America. Tolerating his tantrums and complying with his fantasies was a fair enough price to pay for the perks.

PART II

THE HOUSE OF THE GODS

CHAPTER 8

"There's people!"

Rosita dropped the half-empty tank and looked around, ears straining to catch the direction of the sound. She and Steve were on their second water run together and had assumed the rhythms of a routine already. They worked well together. They chatted as they walked through the shrubbery, keeping an eye out for any big predator, but in general enjoying each other's company.

Tanner stood, his tank in hand, and frowned.

"Sounds like a lot of people," he said.

"Ahoy!" she shouted, her voice echoing along the creek. "Help!"

Steve shook his head. "This is weird."

"Weird how? Can't we climb up a tree and see?"

They looked up at the double canopy of interlaced branches. There was a lower roof of interlacing branches, and then, about ten feet higher, the tops of the trees themselves formed a solid cover.

"Wouldn't see anything anyway," Steve said.

The sound was growing stronger. "They are coming this way anyway." She smiled. "Ahoy, there! We are here!"

"Who are they?" he asked. "Where do they come from?"

It was a dozen voices talking together. More than a dozen. Definitely more. A little crowd, their words impossible to get, the continuous rhythm of their conversations going up and down.

"Maybe from down there," she said. She strained her neck to try and see where the mysterious people were. "Some village, or some work site. There's always people working to cut down trees for the Transamazonica, or to clear pastures." She turned to him. "They saw the plane crash, or the smoke from our fire, or were radioed, and they came up here to rescue us."

She cupped her hands around her mouth. "Over here! Ahoy!!"

Steve closed his eyes and lowered his head, his chin on his chest, listening. The volume increased, but the voices remained confused. There was no pattern, no rhythm.

"These are not people," Tanner said, in a low voice.

"What?"

He shook his head and tapped his ear.

They stood in silence, listening, the choir of unintelligible voices coming closer, babbling incessantly, their volume rising.

"Is it German?" Rosita asked.

The idea of a party of a few dozen Germans chatting passionately while they walked through a jungle on top of a five-thousand feet plateau smack in the middle of the Amazon was clearly absurd.

"Animals?" Tanner said.

"Talking animals?" she asked, giving him a look. "Parrots?"

"You ever heard a flock of seagulls?"

"Wasn't there a band...?"

"Or ducks," he said. He grasped her wrist and pulled her to the edge of the clearing.

"What are you doing?"

"That idea about climbing," he said, "might be good. Up you go."

Rosita looked at him, and then at the tree.

"Why?"

"Caution."

"You scared of seagulls?"

The sound was now loud and close enough for them to pick out single honking, quacking calls. The brushes were rustling, branches snapping as the animals approached.

"Humor me?"

"Why don't you go first?" she asked him, hands on her hips.

"Because you are smaller. I can push you up, and then you can help me climb."

She snorted and let him help her up the tree.

"Hands off my bum, you oaf!"

#

There were dozens of the creatures, moving together like a herd, a twisting snake of long serpentine necks and thin flicking tails, slithering red and purple through the green and black of the undergrowth.

Rosita thought of birds, at first, but it was just a moment.

"What are...?"

Steve shushed her. He was holding on for dear life to a branch, yet leaning forward to get a better look at the creatures. He patted his shirt, took out a cellphone, and pointed it to take some photos. The animals were small, bipedal, more or less the size of a big dog—a German Shepherd or a Great Dane. They had lean bodies, long thin necks, and short arms.

The cell phone camera buzzed repeatedly.

The out-riders of the column turned in their direction, chirping, and then went back to join the tribe. The creatures moved through the clearing and crossed the creek, all the while darting their heads this way and that and quacking like ducks.

Rosita squinted, taking in their big yellow eyes, their sharp white teeth, and small but chunky triangular heads. Their hides were spotted in dark russet and blue and purple. There were feather-like tufts of fuzz along their short arms, and on their tails. While the column proceeded on its march, one of them approached with extreme caution Steve's backpack where it lay, and then prodded it with its clawed foot.

One of its fellows chirped, a high sound similar to a bird call, and came closer to look.

Rosita pulled Steve's sleeve again.

He nodded, barely glancing at her. *This is crazy*, he mouthed. She made a face, and he went back to taking photographs.

It took about ten minutes for the herd to pass through, leaving behind a few stragglers, including the one that had been examining their stuff and its small audience. The curious one had rolled the backpack on the ground, managing to open it. It had spilled the contents outside and was now checking each item. It was particularly interested in a single Mars bar that had fallen out of a side pocket. It observed it from all angles, its twittering becoming a whisper. It prodded it with its foot, kicking it a short distance. It followed, swaying with each step, playing soccer with the chocolate.

Then, in a flash, its head darted forward and its jaws closed on it. It worked its mouth, noisily, and then gave a strangulated gasp, and started shaking its head, making a sort of coughing sound. It jumped and kicked and rolled on the floor until it spat a dripping ball of chocolate, caramel and wrapping plastic. It hissed nastily and backed away from it. The creature's companions let out a chorus of whistling calls. They circled the half-eaten candy, and finally they left the clearing, speeding to reunite with the rest of their herd.

Silence hung heavily on the clearing for long minutes, only broken by the gurgling of the brook and the brushing of the leaves in the breeze.

Then, "Those were fucking dinosaurs!" Rosita blurted.

Steve Tanner just nodded, too dazed to speak.

#

"A flock," Tanner corrected her.

Rosita gave him the eye. "A flock?"

He was busy putting his stuff back into the sack.

"That clade of dinosaurs are the ancestors of birds, so I guess we should call that a flock, not a herd. A flock of theropods."

"Gasteropods?"

He sighed. "Theropods. Coelophysids, by the look of them. Or maybe a murder."

"A murder?"

"Some birds are counted in murders. Crows, for instance."

"Yeah, whatever." She picked up the water tank. "I mean, they didn't look so dangerous, right? The little fellow got stumped with a Mars bar."

"Didn't you see those teeth?" Tanner grimaced. "Those were not the teeth of a candy muncher. Those little fellows are carnivores."

"Shit!" She let go of her tank with a splash. "We better leave this stuff here," she said.

"Uh?"

She hurried to his side. "I guess we should warn the others, right? Make it fast, too. I mean, those were pretty small, but I did see that movie, you know..."

Tanner stood. "You are absolutely right," he said. "Let's move it."

#

"Fuck, man! They think we are fucking porters or something?"

George stood on a small mound, his hands deep in his pockets, and looked around.

Following careful observation, they had determined the luggage from the plane was strewn over an area of about one square mile. Here a red Samsonite trolley lay abandoned in the undergrowth, there a LowePro camera bag hung from a low branch, swaying gently, a small blue and red bird perching on it. One of the bags had exploded, and assorted lingerie, silk rags and other items festooned the lower canopy of the jungle.

Terri picked up a red high-heeled pump and then straightened with a sigh. Maria's, probably.

"You could lend us a hand," she told George.

She was feeling sticky with sweat, she was thirsty, and there was a hollow knot of anxiety in her stomach that the sight of the search plane had not been enough to untie. The mosquitoes were eating her alive.

George laughed. "Yo, bitch! Let me enjoy my vacation."

Dylan chuckled, and she stared daggers at him. "And you let him talk to me like that?"

George grinned. "Touchy bitch!"

"You know how he's like," Dylan said.

"Yes, I always knew he was a useless prick." She threw the shoe at Dylan, hitting him in a shoulder. "But I thought you were different!"

She turned and retraced her steps towards the wreck, Dylan following her, mumbling soothing nonsense.

George watched them go, shaking his head. "Chicks these days," he said.

He found the red shoe where it had landed under a shrub and bent to pick it up.

#

"C'mon, honey," Dylan said, his hand closing on Terri's arm.

She shrugged him off. "Fuck you!" she said.

He sighed.

"Listen," he tried to sound reasonable, "I know this vacation is not going as planned..."

She stopped and turned to him, staring, then laughed. "Not going as planned?!" She opened her arms, embracing the forest around them. "Not going as planned?! We crashed in the middle of the fucking jungle, you fool!"

Dylan shifted his weight from one foot to the other.

Terri sneered at him. "Man, aren't you pathetic!"

He opened his mouth to speak, but right then George's screams echoed through the trees.

"What...?"

Cursing, Terri pushed Dylan out of the path and ran back to where they had left their friend. Around them, the jungle erupted in a chorus of animal calls.

#

George was sitting on the ground, holding his wrist and screaming his head out. He was as pale as a rag, his green jersey splattered with blood.

Terri knelt down by his side. He thrashed when she placed a hand on his shoulder and kept screaming, wide eyes staring at her without seeing. His right hand was a ruin of raw flesh, blood pouring from a long gash.

Dylan rushed into the small clearing, and started blurting questions. With a fiery oath, Terri slapped George in the face, hard.

The young man stopped screaming and looked at her, dazed.

"Shut the fuck up," she said, turning to Dylan, "and go fetch Doctor

Barillier."

"Who?"

"Sandra, the one whose ass you were staring at last night!"

He babbled.

"Move it, you dork, or your bosom buddy's gonna bleed to death!"

She pulled off her tee and wrapped it around George's maimed hand. He was starting to tremble, his lips purple, his pupils dilated.

"George, look at me," she started, trying to remember what she had learned at summer camp ten years ago about treating shock. Lay him down, prop his legs up. Or something.

#

Sandra and Jack Tanner crashed through the foliage, Dylan hot on their heels, panting.

"What happened?" Sandra asked, kneeling by Terri's side.

"He was attacked by an animal," Terri said.

George rolled on his back, his right hand wrapped in a bloodstained rag, his left clutching his right wrist. Sandra unzipped the first aid bag.

"It was a lizard," he said.

Sandra traded a glance with Terri. The younger woman shrugged.

Sandra undid the makeshift bandage and hid a grimace.

Jack was hovering behind her and whistled softly, trying to catch the boy's attention. "What sort of lizard?" he asked.

He snapped his fingers in front of George's face, forcing him to look up. "A lizard?" Jack asked again.

"Y-yes..."

"Look at me, George," Jack said. "What kind of lizard was it? Was it an iguana?"

Sandra nodded to herself and looked closer at the gash in the boy's hand.

"I was picking up the shoe," George said. "Fucker was hiding in the bush. Fucker bit my hand."

He squealed when Sandra sprayed his hand with disinfectant.

"Are you sure it wasn't a snake? What did it look like?" Jack asked.

George shook his head. "As big as a chicken. Red, with stripes."

"I'll have to stitch the wound," Sandra said.

George looked at her in horror.

"You won't feel anything," she promised. From the bag, she picked a pair of small pliers, then glanced at Jack. He nodded.

"Tell me more about this lizard," Tanner said, leaning closer. "Did you do anything to scare it?"

George's eyes widened. "Me? Scare it? Shit, man..."

Sandra stabbed him with a syringe, and proceeded to clean the skin, moving around the wounds with a piece of gauze.

"Is it going to be okay?" the boy asked, his voice breaking. He was pale as a rag, and his voice was thick. Sandra nodded, but he was already gone.

Jack looked around. Dylan held Terri, and the noise in the jungle had somewhat subsided. He noticed the red shoe on the ground a few feet away.

"A red lizard," he said to himself.

#

"Good show," Sandra said.

Jack turned to her. "Don't know what you mean."

She grinned. "Distracting the kid while I fixed his hand."

He shrugged. "I was only curious about the lizard."

They were going back to the plane, Dylan carrying the sleeping George on his shoulders in a fireman carry, and Terri walked by his side in her sports bra and a morose face.

"What do you think?" Jack asked.

"About what?"

"About the red striped lizard."

She made a face. "I'm no expert on Amazonian fauna."

"Me neither," Tanner said. "Wrong brother. But?"

She glanced at Dylan, George, and Terri, making sure they were out of earshot. "But whatever it was," she said, "it bit off two fingers."

Jack stopped. "You didn't—"

"He was scared enough."

She pulled a kerchief out of her pocket and unwrapped it on the palm of her left hand, showing him the contents. Two short chips of bone rolled on the blood-stained cloth.

"Urgh!" he said.

"Third and fourth finger. Bit right through the first phalanx, cutting neatly through the bone," she said, prodding the broken bones. "Then it bit again, but was unable to rip away the thumb. Whatever it was, your red lizard has quite the jaws."

CHAPTER 9

"Dinosaurs?"

Mike stared at Steve and Rosita.

"Yes," Tanner said. "Theropods, to be precise."

The others looked at the two explorers like they were mad.

"Listen," Jack said, stepping forward. "These dinos of yours, they happen to be the size of a soccer ball, red, striped, and with sharp teeth?"

Behind him, Sandra Barillier cursed under her breath.

Steve Tanner arched an eyebrow. "Coelophysids tend to be larger than that," he said. "And those we saw were larger."

He pulled out his cellphone and handed it to his brother. "Say as large as a large dog."

"But you got the color, more or less," Rosita said. "And the teeth."

"Shouldn't these things be extinct?" Jack asked, browsing wide-eyed through the images. Sandra and Mike were peeping over his shoulder.

"What are you guys talking about?" Dylan said, waving his arms around.

"We're talking about the lizard that made a snack of your pal."

Steve frowned. "There's been an attack?"

"Red, striped little bastard, the size of a chicken," Jack said. "Bit two fingers off George."

Mike sat down heavily. "Those rescue guys better make it fast," he said.

Dylan cuddled Terri. "Yes, George. What happened to him—"

"What happened to him," Mike said, "is also part of the bad news."

"Well, there's wild animals," Barreto said. "We sort of expected that, right? We knew it. Tepui or whatever, this is the Amazon. Dinosaurs or leopards, it does not make much difference."

Steve Tanner stared at him, goggle-eyed. The guy was crazy. Now he was sure.

Mike looked at Steve and Rosita. "You sure about this, right?"

Now Rosita's eyes grew wider. "Sure? We all saw the damn beasts, how sure can we be? We've got photos, for Chrissakes."

Everybody started talking at the same time. Steve pulled out his cellphone again.

#

"Now, I hate to ask things like these," Jack Tanner said, when finally the questions and exclamations subsided, "but shouldn't these creatures be, like, dead? Extinct?"

His brother shrugged. "The fact that they are here shows that they are not."

"Yeah, thanks so much," Rosita said. She prodded the fire with a stick.

"What I mean is, we have new data and we must revise our models. That's the way science works."

"So they died everywhere else but not here. Like in that movie," Dylan said. "This thing is gonna be huge."

"Yeah, right," Rosita replied without turning. "We'll make the cover of National Geographic."

"There's one thing I don't get," Sandra said. "I mean, the dinosaurs' extinction is a global event, right? Triggered by a meteor impact. Not far from here, if I remember correctly."

"In the Gulf, by the Yucatan peninsula, yes." Steve nodded. "More likely a comet core than a meteor, but yes, that's the most popular theory. There's also—"

"Exactly," she cut him short. "Now, the idea is this meteor or comet caused a big," she gestured, "firestorm or something, and then a nuclear winter, and that killed off the dinos—"

"It's a little more complicated than that. Acid rain—"

"Okay, bear with me. I'm a doctor, not a paleontologist. My point is, how come they are still thriving in this place?"

Steve Tanner ran a hand through his hair, taking a deep breath. "I don't know."

Dylan snickered. "Some scientist."

Steve stared at him from underneath heavy eyelids.

"You are going to regret that, kid." Jack grinned. "We all are."

"I don't know," Steve repeated, glancing at Dylan and turning to the doctor. "But I can make a few educated guesses. First of all, we are not one hundred percent certain about the impact, the so-called Nemesis event, being the true or exclusive dino killer. Considering what we have just discovered, maybe the Shiva hypothesis is the right one."

"Shiva?" Rosita asked with a grimace.

"It is an alternative model that connects the Great Death at the Cretaceous-Tertiary boundary with the massive volcanic effusions of the Deccan Traps, in India. The idea being that the gases released during many thousand years of continuous volcanic activity somehow saturated the atmosphere, and then poisoned or suffocated the dinosaurs. And changed the climate."

"But then why—?" Sandra asked again.

"If the Deccan gases really acted on the climate, causing a collapse of the food chain, then this pocket of the world could have survived by some freak of atmospheric circulation. Also, we are very high above sea level. Maybe this, plus some quirk in the atmospheric flow caused this area to be spared. There were some studies done by the Pentagon in the '70s—"

"And nobody ever noticed?" Maria Barreto asked. "For thousands of years?"

Tanner shrugged. "Tepuis are isolated entities, difficult to access. They do not form a connected range. This makes them host to hundreds of endemic plant and animal species, some of which are found only on one tepui, and not on the next. Each of these mesas is an ecosystem unto itself, and it's not like there's much coming and going hereabouts. Only a century has passed since we became really aware of these places, and only twenty-five years since we started climbing and visiting regularly."

"But basically you don't know," Dylan said with a grin. Terri shook her head.

"There are more urgent things I'd like to know," Mike said, lighting a cigarette. "Like, how dangerous are these things?"

"And are they edible?" Dylan chuckled. Terri punched him in the arm.

Steve cast a pitying glance at the young man, then lifted his shoulders. "The ones we saw are carnivorous and obviously gregarious. But all things considered, you are talking to the wrong guy."

"Exactly," Jack said, moving closer to the fire. The air was growing colder.

"Come again?" Rosita turned to Steve. "Aren't you a geologist?"

"I'm supposed to be a stratigrapher." She frowned, he grinned. "A geologist that studies stratified rocks and the fossils within."

"Right, so you know these beasts."

"As much as you know the taste of a Big Mac from the photo on a Burger King ad." He paused and took a sip of water. "Nobody ever saw these creatures alive. They, as it was rightly pointed out already, are supposed to be extinct. Dead for sixty-five million years. We have models and reconstructions and hypotheses, but nobody has ever met them in the flesh. Until now."

Jack cut him short. "They bite, and there's a lot of them," he said. "That's all we need to know right now, and I'd say we are better off keeping out of their way."

Steve grunted. "Yes, what he said."

"But," Hernan Barreto said. He leaned forward, the fire playing with shadows on his lean face. "We are the dominant species, right? The super-predator. We are at the top of the pyramid. We have the advantage of evolution. They are obsolete—they died out millions of years ago, you said so yourself."

"Well, here they did not," Steve replied. "Obsolescence is not that straightforward."

"What do you mean?"

"Have you seen mammals around? Or birds?"

Hernan looked around. His wife came to his rescue. "Well, I'm sure I saw some birds in the sky today..."

"And we've all heard them chirping in the trees," Mike added.

"Are you sure they were birds? The animals we met today," Steve nodded at Rosita, "are the ancestors of the birds."

Barreto lifted a hand, palm up. "Well, we descend from apes, and apes are—"

"No, we and certain apes descend from common ancestors. And he's gone, because we are here, with the chimps and gorillas. It usually works that way."

"Well, birds could come from the forest down below," Jack said. "They fly, you know."

"I saw a flying lizard," Terri said.

They all turned to her.

"Where?" Steve asked.

"When?" asked Jack.

"As we flew through the storm. A moment before we crashed. It was big and flew by our side. Big wings flapping in the rain, big teeth. Like a dragon."

Mike and Rosita stared at each other. "I didn't see anything," the pilot said.

"Tell us something we don't know." Dylan chuckled.

In a heartbeat Jack was gripping him by the front of his Big Bang Theory T-shirt, and pulling him to his feet. "Listen, you dickhead," he hissed, his face two inches from the boy's. "What's your problem, huh?"

Dylan thrashed and tried to escape, but the logger was holding him one inch off the ground. "Let me go!"

"I've had a very long day, and it's been a very bad week," Jack said, his voice very low. "I lost my job, had to move across a continent. My plane crashed. I'm stranded on top of a mountain. With dinosaurs. And I'm pretty sure we all have enough problems, and we don't need some smartass frat boy playing the joker, okay?"

He let him go, and Dylan sat down on the ground.

"You are crazy, man!"

Jack stared at him. "Yes, I'm crazy." In the light from the fire, half his face was in darkness. "Don't make me mad."

Inside the broken fuselage, George woke up screaming. Dylan and Terry decided it was best to go and see their friend. Sandra followed them, picking up her medical kit.

Rosita watched them go, then turned to Steve. "Anything else we should know about these creatures?"

Steve shook his head. "It's not like this is a normal situation," he said. "I mean, first, what we know about these creatures comes from inference based on fossils. As I said, we actually never saw them in real life."

"Until today."

"Yep. And second, these are not the dinos from the fossil record. They're not the ones from the books. At least, they shouldn't be."

"Evolution," Mike said.

"Exactly. Sixty-five million years is a lot of time, even for living fossils in a very stable environment. It's impossible these creatures did not change, in some way. So all the bets are off. But they are dangerous."

"In other words," Rosita said, "keep clear of the bit with the teeth, and when in doubt climb a tree."

"Essentially, yes. But there's more than that," Steve said. "And it takes us back to the dominant species and the evolutionary advantage story. Natural selection is a complicated machine. The environment selects the organisms, but the organisms also modify the environment. It's called co-evolution. The fast gazelle forces the lion to be faster, and also the other way around. This means that this place has had a number of millions of years for every single bit of its machinery to fine-tune itself to the general pattern."

Rosita shook her head, but it was Maria Barreto who spoke. "I don't understand."

Steve took a deep breath. "What I mean is that everything here is adapted. Every tree, every bush or fern, every animal, insect, flower. They are all part of a perfect machine that works like clockwork, that survives and thrives, that evolves under the pressure of natural selection. The plants evolved under the selective pressure of the herbivores, which evolved under the selective pressure of the big predators, and this modeled the environment. Everything is fine-tuned, and we have no place in it. We are the extraneous organism, we are the outsiders, the bounders. It's not just the dinos—and incidentally we only saw small ones. This is a very limited environment, a very small box. But everything in this box is potentially working against us."

"In other words," Jack Tanner said, "if help doesn't come fast, we are screwed."

CHAPTER 10

While the others settled down for the night, Sandra sat down with Mike, Rosita, and the Tanners.

"The news of the local fauna distracted us from the original plan to collect and inventory our resources," she said, waving a notebook.

"How does it look?" Mike asked.

"We are not that bad off," she said, checking her notes. "We have emergency rations, enough for about a week, and a discreet supply of comfort food: chocolate, cookies, stuff like that. Not healthy, but good for morale. We also have rain protection for everyone, and covers and clothes. Two or three suitcases are still missing, but nothing essential. We have an inflatable lifeboat and twelve, no, make it eleven flares. Also," she followed the list with the tip of her finger, "two first-aid kits, and two working laptops. A geologist's pick—"

"That's a hammer, actually," Steve said.

"Whatever. And a folding spade. Then, two pairs of tough leather work gloves, a bottle of Bowmore whiskey," she turned to Mike, "I commend your choice, Captain."

He bowed.

"Two boxes of Danish butter biscuits, four flashlights, a big bag of weed and a gun, with two full clips."

Mike did a double take. "What?"

"I might add that the owners of the weed and the gun respectively insisted for me to give them back their property." She chuckled. "They could have offered to share."

"Why would you share a gun?" Jack grinned. Then he shook his head. "Okay," he said, "the two bros and the chick were carrying the ganja. Who was packing iron?"

Sandra turned to him. "Actually, I think the weed was another thing Terri was not informed of, judging by the way she chewed her boyfriend's head off."

Mike chuckled and slapped a hand on his cheek. "They tried to smuggle drugs into Venezuela."

"Well, mine was hardly the bust of the century. Based on my experience, it's the standard recreational supply for two college-level imbeciles."

"And the gun?"

"Mister Barreto claims it is registered and he was carrying it because Caracas is a dangerous place."

"Right, then bring an extra gun into it," Jack said.

Rosita gave a "told you so" look at Steve.

"Which explains why he was crying about his right to privacy earlier on," Mike said.

"Yeah," Jack said, "and why he wanted his bag so badly. Sure, I'd never seen a bloke so attached to his socks."

"What caliber are his socks?" Steve asked.

Sandra looked first at Jack and then at Steve. "Are you kids always so flippant?"

"Only when guns and drugs are involved."

"Or secluded plateaus inhabited by dinosaurs."

The doctor shook her head. "Anyway, now that we know that help is on its way," she said, "we just need to sit tight and wait. Keep an eye out for those big lizards, and try and enjoy our stay."

"Which means we can hit the whiskey and the Danish cakes," Jack said. "In moderation."

"I'd rather stay sober," Steve said. "And if you don't mind I'll take an early night, because tomorrow will hopefully be a clear day and—"

Mike turned to Steve. "And you are not going out there to study those things."

"But…"

"No buts, mister. You can come back later, bring a camera, a film crew, Steven frigging Spielberg himself, you name it. But right now, we stay put."

"We actually have found my bag of cameras…"

"No. As I said, you can take full credit for the discovery, and then come here with a troop from Discovery Channel, from National Geographic or People Magazine. You can come back here and build a theme park, for all I care. But right now, we wait here for the Venezuelans to come and pick us up. The kid lost two fingers. Let's try and keep our losses at that. No need to run any extra risk."

Rosita stood and stretched. "I second that motion." She looked at the sky. She yawned. "And now I'll go find myself a place to sleep."

#

Terri felt like her head was full of tissue. She and the guys were shacked up at the back of the plane, sitting on the floor. She took a deep sigh and handed the joint back to Dylan. He took a puff and handed it to George.

George tried to pick it with his right hand, then cursed and used his left instead.

"Two fingers!" he blurted, breathing out smoke.

"You'll have a story to tell," Dylan said. "Fatso there said this is unprecedented... urgh, first time ever. You were attacked by a goddamn dino, man! Blockbuster movie stuff, but for real. We're gonna make the news. They're gonna make a movie about it and get Vin Diesel to play your part."

He passed the weed back to Terri, who filled up her lungs again. She leaned back into the bulwark and slowly breathed it out. The voice in her head that kept repeating this was a stupid idea was far and faint and silly. She smiled.

"The little bastard wasn't larger than a dachshund," George was saying. Terri thought the weed made him easy to tolerate, but he still was a prick. She chuckled. He lifted his bandaged hand and stared at it, his eyes red and unfocused.

"I'll find the little sucker and make him pay," he said.

"Yeah, right." Dylan laughed. "George versus the dinosaur."

Terri was reminded of what her friend Stella told her on their first week on campus. Stella had shown her how to roll a spliff, and introduced her to the stuff. She said that weed was like an amplifier. If you are feeling good it makes you feel really good, if you are feeling down it can make you feel really down. And if you feel like an asshole, she reflected...

Terri started giggling. "Two fingers," she said. She let the wet end of the spliff drop on the floor. Dylan was already rolling another.

"Whoa?"

George was staring at her, like she was the one that had bit off his pinky. "The fucking beast crippled me!"

"It could have been worse," she said, a big silly smile spreading on her face. "It could have bit off your pecker."

She and Dylan started laughing.

"Fuck you!"

Dylan wiped tears from his eyes. "We'll have to be careful when we go for a pee, from now on."

He started cackling again.

George told them to go screw themselves. They just laughed, and told him they were thinking about it. He stood and walked unsteadily out of the back of the plane, his good hand deep into his pants pocket, the bandaged one cradled against his chest.

#

"Wake up."

Terri squinted. Her head was like a block of wood. She sat up and pushed her hair away from her face. "What now?"

"George is gone."

She felt a shiver and put her arms around her body. Dylan looked worried. "Where has he gone?"

"Dunno. Out there. Looking for his fingers." He giggled.

She looked out. The early rays of the sun were turning the sky a pale gray. The air was cool, and there was a faint mist hanging over the vegetation. It was beautiful. "We have to find him."

"We can't tell the others. They'd start lecturing us."

They tiptoed to where the luggage and the water had been arranged. "Are you sure about this?" he asked.

Terri picked up her old messenger bag and slipped two bottles of water in it. "We'll need food, too."

Dylan picked up his backpack and took two bottles of water in turn.

Terri handed him four slim silver packages. "What's this shit?" he asked.

She shrugged. "Emergency rations," she said.

Dylan unwrapped one and sniffed it. Then took a bite. He turned, munching happily, and exited the wreck. Outside the air was still cold, but already the humidity was rising. They looked one way and then the other.

"Any idea of where he might have gone?"

Terri pointed south. "Back to where he was attacked," she said.

She arranged the bag strap on her shoulder and let him follow her in silence. He dropped the rations wrapper and started fumbling with another.

CHAPTER 11

George hefted the wrench and tiptoed toward the moving bush. He wasn't really sure of where he was, but he knew he had finally found what he had been looking for. "Come to me, you fucker," he whispered, a nasty grin on his face.

The chirping sound came again, and the rustling of leaves.

George moved closer.

"Come, come, come, come," he chanted. "Let me give you what you deserve, you little fucker—"

The rustling and the twittering sound moved, the creature going deeper into the undergrowth. George pursued, taking long steps and pushing the foliage out of his way with his bandaged hand.

"Two fingers, you bastard," he said through his teeth, trying to catch a glimpse of his adversary.

He whistled, a modulated sound, like he was wolf-whistling a chick.

The rustling stopped and an interrogative tweet sounded.

With a leer, George whistled again, and again the creature called back. The bushes moved as the animal drew closer.

"Curious little fucker," George said. "Come to Uncle George..."

He slapped the wrench on the palm of his bandaged hand. It hurt, but the pain was muffled and far away, just a faint reminder of the reason why he wanted to get his hands on the creature and beat it to a pulp. He whistled for a third time.

The response was a long and articulated series of chirps and peeps, rising and falling in tone and volume. Then the creature came out of the vegetation. George took a step back.

This was not the red striped lizard he had met before. This was larger, more or less the size of a big turkey, its body long and slick, with a thin tail that whipped this way and that, flailing the animal's sides as it moved its head back and forth, staring with large yellow eyes at the human. It was a reddish-brown in color, with twin stripes running along its sides, one black, one yellow. It stretched its long snakelike neck, and once again emitted his whistling call, its mouth opening to reveal rows of thin, sharp conic teeth. A crest of dazzling emerald-green feathers ran down its spine.

George looked around.

Was he hearing things? No, something moved in the bushes.

He lifted his bandaged hand in a placatory gesture. "Good boy," he said, like he was facing a hostile dog.

The small dinosaur chirruped and drew its head back, studying him.

George took two steps back.

A second animal joined the first, its head moving up and down, like a machine's. Its skin was paler than the first, its foot-talons longer, its feathers thicker.

George took a deep breath. The weight of the wrench in his hand was no longer reassuring. He turned sharply to the right. There were more of the beasts in the bushes. They were moving. They were all around him. He caught flashes of their rusty skin, glimpses of their twisting tails, hints of yellow eyes glowing, observing him from the shadows.

Another step back, knees slightly flexed, ready to sprint and run away. The two lizards standing in front of him stepped forward, following his retreat, their eyes on him. What had the fat man said? As smart as chimps?

"Fuck!" he said.

He turned left, just in time to catch a glimpse of one of the animals as it jumped at him, talons outstretched. Then the thing was clawing at his face, screeching, calling its friends, and soon the animal calls were so loud they covered George's screams as they died out in a wet, gory gurgle.

CHAPTER 12

It was raining lightly in Tama-Tama. The air in the hangar was hot and sticky. The choppers had been parked and checked. The men were smoking and drinking coffee when Hans Schneider entered. They greeted him, a broken chorus of rough voices.

He returned the greeting with a nod. Imposing despite his nondescript pants and short-sleeved shirt, he was tall, fair-haired, and stone-faced. He gestured for them to settle down and poured himself a cup of coffee. He grimaced. Too hot and very bad.

"Okay, gentlemen," he said. He scanned their faces with flinty eyes. "Time being critical, I'll go through this rather quickly."

The guys found places to sit or lounge, while he placed his laptop on top of a crate and started it up.

"Wow, boss, you've gone all hi-tech!"

There was sparse laughter.

Schneider didn't laugh.

They stopped laughing.

The system went online with a buzz. Two clicks, and a square green blot appeared on the screen.

"Can somebody turn out the lights?" someone called.

"We're in a fucking hangar, Mick."

"Shit, man. I hadn't noticed that!"

Schneider adjusted the controls on his computer, and the blot resolved itself into a satellite image of a stretch of jungle.

"Okay, this is the target area," Schneider said, tapping the rim of the screen. "The place is called Tampali Tepui. It's a plateau to the south and east of here. Elevation, seven thousand feet, and surrounded by ten thousand square kilometers of jungle. Venezuela, Bolivar province."

"A cat litter," Mick said.

Schneider could sympathize with the sentiment.

More images followed of a blocky-looking mountain, its sheer cliffs white in the sun, topped by a fuzz of green.

"The area is formally parkland, UNESCO heritage, the works," Schneider went on. "No population worth mentioning, no roads, no landing strips, no security cameras, no social justice warriors. The whole sector is jointly managed by Venezuela and Brazil, and requires special permits to access."

"And do we have them?"

Mick was clearly willing to be the joker of the team.

"We don't need them."

Some of the men laughed, another slowly clapped his hands.

The photo of an ugly airplane swam on the screen.

"This bird went down there two days ago. Civilian flight out of Peru, eight passengers, two crew members. We assume that at least some of the passengers survived the crash."

Another picture.

The guys cheered, whistled and cat-called.

Schneider glanced at the photo of the dark-skinned, raven-haired woman in a red dress and the young man grinning awkwardly at the camera. In full display on the woman's impressive cleavage was a simple silver cross, hanging from a thin silver chain.

"What a babe!" Mick was at it again.

"I guess she's taken already," the guy sitting by his side said.

"Damn. Does she have a sister, boss?"

More laughter.

Schneider went on, impassive. "These are the two individuals we are to locate and, if alive, apprehend."

"'T'would be a pity had missy there bought the farm."

"Twenty men to pick up a cool chick?" another man asked. Schneider glanced at him. Alan D. Ortega. They had worked together in the past, in places whose name it was his job to forget. Levelheaded, cautious, a pain in the ass. "And what if they are dead?"

Schneider looked at him. "Then we'll shift to Plan B."

"Which is?"

"None of your business right now, Ortega."

More laughter.

Schneider closed his laptop. End of briefing.

One of the guys, a big man with a scar on his chin, put up a hand. "What about the other people on that plane?"

Schneider allowed himself a thin smile.

"When the rescue teams get there, they will find that there were no survivors."

"Somebody will notice there's two people missing," Ortega observed.

"Or the bullet holes."

"No one will be missing."

The men were silent, all mirth drained from them.

"The chick in red, too?" Mick asked.

Schneider did not waste time answering. Juggling the short notice and the need for secrecy, he had selected them with care, hand-picking men who would not squirm at the idea of killing civilians. But he guessed they needed some time to adjust to the idea anyway.

He looked at his wristwatch.

"We take off one hour before dawn. Get some bunk time."

CHAPTER 13

"Jack..."

Jack Tanner started awake. "Uh?"

"Trouble," said his brother. "The kids are gone."

Jack cursed and rubbed what was left of sleep from his eyes. He ran his fingers through his beard and stood, stretching with a groan. The others had assembled outside, by the open end of the hull.

"There's some stuff missing," Mike said. "They took four bottles of water, some of the emergency rations, and the largest of our wrenches."

Jack grinned. "A wrench?"

"Yeah. And don't ask me why."

"Let's say we have conclusive evidence they were stoned," Rosita said.

"Stupid idiots," Hernan Barreto hissed.

Sandra emerged from the plane carrying her medical kit. "Any idea of where they went?"

"I get a hunch they went in the same direction they went yesterday," Steve said.

Jack slapped his hand against the bent metal of the plane's hull and cursed. "Makes perfect sense. You are lost in the jungle, surrounded by prehistoric fauna, waiting for help, what else to do but smoke a spliff and then go for a walk."

Steve shook his head. "They took four bottles," he said.

Sandra arched an eyebrow. "You doing your Sherlock thing again?"

"I would, but there's no time. We should go and bring the three idiots back."

"Sounds like a plan," Jack said. "So, three parties. One to the south, the other to the east, to the creek. The third to the east along the crest out there, just in case."

"And we don't go alone," Mike added.

Rosita moved to Steve's side. "We can go back to the creek, and make a wide curve coming back. We can cover a lot of terrain, and we sort of know that area, what with our water forays and all."

Sandra stared at her.

"What?"

The doctor shook her head and smiled. "Nothing."

"I'm going south," Jack volunteered. "As we are at it, we can go the distance and retrieve the ELT from the tail cone. We want the rescue team to find us fast, so we better keep the ELT close."

"And I'm coming with you," Mike said.

"Which leaves us girls to go hiking uphill, I guess," Sandra said to Maria Barreto.

"And you are leaving me here? Alone?" Hernan's voice was high with fear.

"It's not like anything is going to happen," Mike said. "And you've got a gun, right?"

"And a broken arm!"

Maria linked arms with Hernan. "I would rather stay with my husband," she said, flashing her dazzling smile. "He can't use his left arm and needs my help."

"It's not like we'll be away for the whole day," Sandra said. "The guys can't be more than two or three miles from here."

"And Sandra can't go alone," Jack said.

"Nobody has to go," Hernan said. They stared at him.

"I mean, the rescue teams will be here in a few hours, right?" Barreto said. "And there are monsters out there. Dangerous. You said that. Why should we risk our lives? Those three idiots, as you called them yourselves, deserve anything that happens to them."

There was a long, awkward moment of silence.

"And they'll probably be back on their own," Maria said, clearly trying to salvage the situation. But it was too late. She placed a hand on the man's shoulder.

"It's your basic Darwinist theory, isn't it?" Barreto asked Steve Tanner. "Survival of the fittest."

The big man opened his mouth, and then shut it, with a sigh. It was his brother that answered back. "Survival of the one that stays put, and screw everybody else?"

Barreto gave him a look of pity. "I just don't see why we should risk our lives to take care of people who clearly are not interested in taking care of themselves."

"Two teams," Jack said, turning his back on him. "Steve and Rosy to the east, me and Mike to the south."

Mike O'Reilly stared at Hernan Barreto. "No," he said. "You take Sandra. The kids might need a doctor, after all."

"You?"

"I'll take a jaunt to that ridge you mentioned," Mike said, his eyes still on Barreto. "Might be a nice vantage point."

"Alone?" Sandra said. "You said we should go in pairs."

Mike lifted his shoulders. "Change of plans."

"But..."

"I'll take a flare. Anything happens, you'll see my signal."

"Everybody might as well take one along," Rosita said. She took two from the supply bag, and handed one to Jack, pocketing the other.

Jack gazed at Mike for a moment. "Okay," he said finally, slipping the flare in a pocket. "Let's move it."

#

"Tell me about the four bottles of water," Rosita said.

"What?"

"The story about the four bottles of water. Sandra talked about Sherlock. Tell me."

Steve shrugged. "Three people go on a hike. How many bottles of water do they bring?"

Rosita stopped, leaning on a tree. "Three, one each," she said. "Or six, two apiece."

"Exactly."

She looked around, spotted a fallen tree trunk and sat on it. The air thick with humidity made breathing a chore. "So what do you deduce?"

"I dunno. But I think two of them left with the water and the supplies, the other left alone with the wrench."

She nodded. "George, wrench, Romeo and Juliet, water and stuff."

"Sounds reasonable. George wakes up in a daze——"

"Stoned out of his small brain."

"And decides to go dino hunting. He's got a score to settle, or something. Looks for a weapon, grabs the wrench, and goes."

"His pals find out, and decide to go after him. They pick some provisions for the road."

"Bingo."

Rosita undid her ponytail and shook her head. She passed her fingers through her hair. "And where does this leave us?"

"In the middle of nowhere," Steve replied.

"A wet, sticky nowhere."

"But it tells us the guys are in trouble. If nothing else, because George went out looking for a dinosaur. He might actually find it."

"And he's stoned out of his head," Rosita said again. She did her ponytail again, and then she placed a hand on the trunk to help herself up. The trunk moved under her fingers.

She turned, screamed, jumped away.

A ten-inch-long creature, its segmented body a coppery brown, wrapped itself around her wrists. She screamed again.

"Take it off me!"

She stood, stumbled and fell sitting on the ground. She tried to pull the slick carapace away, but it just hurt her more. A seething mass of shiny creatures, their armor shining red-brown in the diffused sunlight, moved from the trunk towards her. She squealed and tried to get out of their way.

Steve was by her side, holding her up, and pacing rapidly back. The creature looked like a big bracelet, hugging the lower arm of the woman. Grimacing, he tried to push his fingers between her skin and the thing's carapace. A rivulet of blood ran along the back of Rosita's hand, and she hissed a cuss word. She was pale, her eyes dilated. Steve patted his fisherman vest pockets, pulled out a zippo lighter and snapped it open. He brushed the flame along the scaly body. The thing shuddered, and dropped away. It rolled on its back, balled up and unfurled again, hobbling away on its multitude of tiny legs. He squashed it with the heel of his boot. It made a sick sound.

Rosita was reciting a rosary of obscenities. He picked her up, ignoring her squeal, and holding her in his arms he jumped on top of a flat boulder. There he put her down. The crawling creatures crowded around the squashed remains of their companion.

"Let me look!"

There was a circle of triangular cuts on Rosita's wrist, like thumb-tack marks, bleeding profusely. "What if it was poisonous?" she asked.

She was very pale and trembling.

"Venomous," he corrected her.

"What?"

"Poisonous if you eat it, venomous if it injects you."

"Would you just fuck off, please?"

"I see that you are out of your mind with pain." He grinned.

He splashed her wrist with water, then proceeded to clean the cut. "Not swollen, no weird colors. I guess the bastard just drank some of your blood."

"Like a fucking leech." She shuddered. "It had a lot of legs. I felt them rubbing on my skin. Like it was pedaling while he sucked on my blood. Like it was liking it."

He splashed her with peroxide. She cursed again, then took a deep breath. "Dinosaur-grade tick."

"Something like that, yes."

"House of the gods, my ass," she said. "This place is a fucking nightmare. Here, I'll do it."

She took the bandage from his hand and proceeded to wrap her wrist, pulling it tight. Red spots flowered on the white gauze. She did a few more layers.

In the grass, more of the creatures circled the carcass of their mate.

"So you actually don't know those critters, right?"

He turned his hands palms up. "Haven't the faintest."

"Geologist," she snorted. "We better look for those kids."

#

It was really a quick jaunt to the ridge, and Mike enjoyed the energetic walk and the loneliness. He opened his way through the vegetation, walking at a brisk pace but never letting his guard down, always scanning the surroundings. Tanner was right—the vegetation was weird. There were pines and birches and occasionally palm trees.

He tried to push Hernan Barreto to the back of his mind. The man was an arrogant fool, and sinister. Mike had a very bad feeling about him.

The ground rose rapidly, and he had to concentrate on finding hand- and foot-holds as he climbed up. Soon he was high enough to look in that weird, unexpected space sandwiched between the top of the trees and the lower canopy of intertwined branches. It was like a vast, green attic. A big bug buzzed in his direction, hovering for a moment in front of him, fat and iridescent in a beam of light. A green bird—or maybe it was a lizard—intercepted it and disappeared in the foliage.

Mike had a flash of the bug crunched under tiny conical teeth. No, not a bird.

Higher still he climbed, the thin layer of soil making the slope slippery, until he finally rose above the treetops.

The jungle stretched to the horizon, unbroken. Even their landing corridor was not visible from here, hidden by successive curtains of vegetation. There were clouds surrounding the plateau, and it looked like the forest just faded into fluffy whiteness. High in the sky, a big flying shape batted its wings, and then stretched them out, gliding on an updraft. No wonder, Mike thought, nobody had ever seen the strange fauna of this place. The dinosaurs were small and well hidden in the thick of the jungle, or flew high above the clouds. No air survey or satellite imagery could spot them.

In the distance, he saw a flock of flying creatures rise suddenly, like they had been scared by something. The guys looking for the kids, he imagined.

He spent about half an hour there, sitting on a rock, enjoying the panorama and the sun, the breeze making the humidity tolerable. The rescue parties would be back soon, of this he was certain. Just as he was certain that he could wave goodbye to his license. Grounded, bankrupt.

But he guessed that what they had found here would make up for the losses.

He pushed his hands in his pockets and chuckled to himself. Here he was, fifty-four years old, dreaming of TV interviews and easy money.

Time to go back, he thought. Time to connect again with reality.

CHAPTER 14

Finding George had cleared their heads better than a cold shower. They had both thrown up, leaning against trees. Now Terri sat on the ground, pale as a rag, holding a water bottle, while Dylan paced up and down on the trampled grass. Both were doing their best to avoid the sight of the red pile of raw meat that was all that remained of their friend.

Terri looked up, to a branch where a ragged blue T-shirt hung, waving like a flag, a memento of their crash landing. Had it really been just two days back?

"We should go back to the plane," she said.

Dylan looked at her. "You know what they will say!"

"I don't give a damn about what they will say. They'd probably be right."

"What do you mean?"

"They told us it was dangerous. They said we should take care, stay put, stay together."

"They are just full of shit!"

"But George is dead."

She was silent.

"We should bury him," he said finally.

"We don't have the tools."

The wrench George had carried was still there by the remains of his body, splattered with blood. She stood up with a sigh. "Let's go back."

She felt hollow and faint.

"I'm not leaving him here like this," Dylan said, his jaw set.

She surprised herself with a chuckle. "What else could happen to him? You fear somebody will steal his Adidas?"

As in response to her question, a tiny lizard-thing flapped down from a tree branch and perched on George's carcass, nibbling at it. It was blue and emerald, with wings tipped with small claws. Dylan scared it away, shouting and waving his arms.

Something moved in the bushes.

Dylan and Terri froze.

"Good morning, campers," Jack Tanner said with a grin, disentangling himself from the greenery.

Behind him, Sandra stepped up, looking worried. "You two fine?" she asked.

They both nodded and instinctively turned to where George was resting.

Tanner cursed, the smile disappearing. While he turned away, breathing heavily, Sandra crouched down to examine the remains. The boy had been ripped to shreds, his flesh mangled. She had seen something similar in textbooks, photos of people attacked by dog packs, by hyenas. The stench was ugly. She felt her gorge rise, despite her training.

She concentrated on her breathing, keeping her body under control. Her mind shifted in the callous indifference that field surgeons have to develop to survive. A dead body. Rough matter. The ground around the body had been trampled by his friends, but she could still make out the prints of small lizard-like feet. "He was attacked by a pack of them," she said.

"We should bury him," Dylan said.

Jack pulled off his backpack and took out the folding shovel. Sandra stared at him.

"I believe in preparedness," the man said. "I'd have preferred a machete, but this turns out to be the right tool for the job. And we can't leave him like that."

A low growl echoed in the clearing, followed by another.

They looked at each other.

Jack gripped his shovel. "Oh, shit."

#

It was Maria's shout that called them outside.

"My goodness!"

There was a herd of big lumbering lizards, grazing on the broken vegetation of their landing path. A dozen big, rhinoceros-like monsters, with a fan-like shield over their heads, the margin sporting a number of conical spikes.

"They are damn big," Mike said.

"They are beautiful," Maria replied.

They were blue-green, their hides scaly and warty. Their head-shields ranged from bright yellow to orange, the spikes black. They moved slowly across the cleared path, grazing the grasses and sometimes munching on a piece of bark, on a broken branch.

One of them looked up, turned its head this way and that, and then let out a honk, like a broken trumpet. Then he got back to feeding.

"Look at that!"

Maria pointed at a small bird-like thing hopping on the back of one of the large dinosaurs.

Again one of the beasts looked up, made sure that everything was just like before, and let out its honking call. The two men and the woman stood there, looking at this strangely colored herd as it wandered over the path.

"You think they are dangerous?" Hernan asked.

Mike thought he caught a tired glance from Maria, but he just pushed his hands in his pockets and ignored it. "If they are herbivores, they shouldn't be a problem."

One of the things looked at them, its eye as big as a fist, staring. It moved its head, sniffing the air. It gave a short series of honks and moved towards the plane at a slow gait. It was vaguely ridiculous, just as Mike had always considered baby elephants ridiculous. But this was an unknown species. "Maybe we should get inside," Mike said.

He turned just in time to see Hernan Barreto pull out his gun and take aim. The dino came closer, honking like an old Volkswagen Beetle.

"No, you fool!"

The bang echoed over the cleared path and the surrounding forest. They couldn't see where the bullet hit, but the animal let out a shrill wail. All of its companions stopped their grazing and turned towards the plane, while the wounded dino tossed its head and charged.

Hernan Barreto fired two more useless bullets before his wife dragged him inside the wreck. One moment later, the dinosaur slammed into the hull, shaking it like a toy.

"You fucking idiot!" Mike said, trying to keep his balance. He saw the light in Barreto's eyes and the gun in his hand and was sure he was going to shoot him.

Then the Pilatus rocked again, slamming against the rock that had stopped its descent, and the sound of thundering feet became deafening. The cabin shook like in an earthquake. Maria started talking rapidly to Hernan, but there was too much going on for Mike to understand or care about it. But he could get the gist. It was pretty obvious that she was the one that wore the trousers in the Barreto household. Hernan tried haltingly to defend himself, but soon he just looked down, mumbling apologies.

Two of the surviving side windows exploded under the assault. Mike reflected that Hernan Barreto looked like he would have rather welcomed the attention of the bull dinos.

"Look out!"

One of the beasts had circled the wreck and found the back opening. It rammed its head in the cabin, the big orange head shield hitting the ceiling, its beak-like snout pushed between two seats. It leaped forward and its shoulders hit the metal of the hull. Bellowing in fury and frustration, the thing just pushed harder. The structure groaned.

Mike, Maria, and Hernan retreated toward the forward cabin. The monster tried to pull back, but the spikes of its shield were stuck against the ceiling and the walls of the cabin. Thrashing in fury, stuck half in, half out of the plane, the dinosaur let out another deafening trumpet-like sound and pushed again. The metal creaked and the stump of wing resting on the rock face screeched as the wreck started to move.

Mike cursed.

The dino pushed some more, and the plane moved again.

Hernan leveled his gun again, but Mike grabbed his wrist and pulled the weapon down.

"You caused enough trouble already," he had time to say.

Another shove from the dino and the wreck was free of the supporting rock, and it rolled on its side, the broken wing digging in the dirt. They stumbled and fell, Hernan moaning as he landed on his broken arm. The rolling movement dislodged the dinosaur from the back breach, and it retreated, shaking its head and snorting in irritation. Its companions once again pushed against the hull, causing another earthquake.

Then everything was over.

Mike looked out of the porthole, at the herd of garishly colored dinosaurs, grazing peacefully about one hundred yards from the plane. It was like nothing had happened.

"Are they gone?" Maria asked behind him.

"I think they just forgot about us," he replied without turning.

CHAPTER 15

Three huge beasts stalked into the clearing, making a beeline for the remains of George. They settled around it, sniffing the remains and kicking the wrecked body around.

They had massive heads and very short forearms, and their slick bodies were stooped and long-tailed. They were smaller than Jack had expected, maybe fifteen feet. He remembered seeing a skeleton in the British Museum, same head, same teeth, but much larger. These monsters had dripping jaws, and their thick hide was bumpy, a mix of yellow and dark brown. And yet they were impossible to mistake for something else.

"That's a fucking T Rex," Dylan hissed.

The closest beast turned, its growl turning into a sharp chirping sound.

"And they have good hearing," Jack said. "Run!"

They ducked into the undergrowth as the three dinosaurs started after them. They moved in formation, one to the fore and two at the wings, screeching and growling, feet pounding through the vegetation.

They ran breathlessly, Jack taking the lead, pushing branches and bushes out of the way. He used the shovel like a machete, opening the way. Sandra barely kept up with him, Terri and Dylan came last, holding hands. "Let's split!" Jack shouted.

He let the others go deeper into the forest and he held his ground, waving and shouting, trying to attract the attention of the three animals. "This way, you bastards!"

The three Rexes ran to him, then separated. One kept coming straight at him, while the other two moved to the left and the right, diving into the thick of the vegetation.

Jack started running again, zigzagging through the trees, the bushes slapping in his face. He concentrated on pumping with his legs and kept looking forward.

Suddenly the air became heavy with the smell of rotting flesh. Instinctively, he rolled on the left, jumping into a clump of fern-like foliage as a T Rex passed him and tried to snap a bite at him.

He barely had time to get his bearings before the second hunter was upon him, converging from the side. Jack leapfrogged behind a tree, and when the beast pushed its head around the trunk, he slammed the shovel in the side of its head. The serrated margin of the tool bit hard in the beast's right eye. It snorted, retreated and then ran around the tree, but Jack was already running.

#

Sandra crashed through the underbrush, gasping, the sound of the running monster behind her. She jostled around a large tree and tottered on the brink of a fifty feet drop. She grabbed the tree to hold her balance.

In front of her, a gorge cut through the plateau, maybe twenty yards wide. It was filled with mist, its white rock walls covered with a thick layer of vines. Something flew by, squeaking. She got an impression of bright feathers, of small claws at the end of its wings.

The ground-pounding steps of the Rex came closer, like a dull drumming, as the beast slowed and came her way. Sandra turned, staring into the wide open mouth of the monster, its fetid breath choking her. Without thinking, instinct overriding millennia of civilization, she grabbed a vine, and launched herself across the chasm.

Only when she was in mid-flight, the dinosaur roaring its frustration at her, she realized what she was doing. She almost lost her grip. She saw the rock cliff rush at her, closed her eyes, and then the vine she was riding gave and she fell. She hung in the void for an eternity, her blood roaring in her ears. Then she landed on her bum on a thick cushion of ferns, her kit bag exploding and pouring its contents all around her.

#

"Where are they?"

Terri was completely lost, and she wondered what had become of Jack and Sandra.

She and Dylan pushed through the ferns and the shrubs, making what she thought was a lot of noise. Dylan looked around, shushing her. "They probably followed baldy and the blonde. We are safe."

He was walking in a half crouch, like he was trying to make himself smaller, hiding in the undergrowth. His eyes darted around, and he looked like a trapped animal. It was in that moment that Terri realized she was no longer in love with Dylan. She felt a sort of warm feeling, yes, but it was probably compassion. Pity.

She let go of his hand, and stood, watching him dispassionately. What a useless, horrid, self-centered prick, she thought. He stopped and turned to her, an interrogative look on his face. Then the T Rex bit his head off.

Its head came crashing through the foliage and dripping fangs closed over Dylan's head. Then it pushed the body on the ground, pressing it down with its foot, cracking the rib cage with a loud unpleasant sound. It turned to her, chewing.

Terri felt completely empty.

No fear, no panic. She felt like death.

The yellow eyes of the dinosaur fixed on her. It chirped and bent down to tear away a chunk of red meat and rags from the body of her boyfriend. Her ex. And still it stared at her, tilting its head this way and that, a human arm dangling through its teeth.

Terri watched it. The tattoo, the wristwatch.

Like in a dream, she turned on her heels and started running.

#

Sandra tried to get her bearings. The fracture ran more or less north to south, parallel to the edge of the upper plateau. She just had to turn left, and follow the line of the chasm, and she'd come across the creek Rosita and Steve had found, where the stone bathtubs were. And there was a good, clear track from the creek to the plane. No sweat.

She pulled her hair up and fixed it in place with a clip. The forest around her was a silent expanse of green shadows and mist. There were animals calling, and things moved in the undergrowth.

She took a deep breath and started north, reasoning that those unseen beasts were probably as scared of her as she was of them.

#

Mike stared into Hernan Barreto's eyes.

"Hand me that gun, now," he repeated for the third time. The air in the wrecked cabin of the Pilatus was hot and humid and smelled of bodies too closely packed. Barreto just stared back, an insouciant expression on his face, the gun still firmly in his grip.

Mike scowled. "You are going to get us trampled to death, or worse, with your playing John Wayne."

Barreto circled his wife's waist with his splinted arm. "I need this gun to protect my wife."

"Your wife faces no danger," Mike said, looking in her direction in search of support and finding none. "Apart from the dangers in which you can put her in playing with that pistol."

"As I think it was stated already," Barreto said, "you are the last person who should talk about our safety or about dangers."

Mike stepped back, like he had been slapped in the face. "I am responsible for the safety of all passengers, and I have been doing my best—"

"And we've all suffered the consequences of you trying to do your best, and failing."

Mike punched him in the face. It was so fast and unexpected, Barreto never saw it coming. The fist zipped between them and slammed with a satisfactory thud on the younger man's cheekbone.

Barreto's head snapped back, he staggered, and Mike got closer and hit him again, a one-two sequence to the body, and a final uppercut to the chin. Barreto groaned, winded, and fell back. He stumbled, and ended up with his feet in the air, jammed between two seats. The gun fell to the floor, resting on the dirty carpeting of the cabin.

"Leave him alone!" Maria shouted, stepping between them, pushing Mike back. "He's hurt, his arm is broken, you coward!"

Mike snorted. "He was the one with the gun."

He bent, picked it up, and slipped it in his pocket.

"Take care of your invalid," he told her. "And help him grow up."

#

The movement and the chattering in the vegetation grew more intense.

Sandra stopped.

A small creature, perhaps two feet high, jumped out from under a bush and stood in front of her. More of the same, Sandra was sure, were moving among the foliage. She thought of the striped red lizard, of George's devastated corpse. Attack from a pack of small animals. She stared as the creature crouched on its hind legs, its round head tilted to the side.

More sounds, and Sandra half turned to see a second lizard sitting in the path behind her. Both animals were dark blue and orange, with iridescent scales along the sides of their bodies. Small head, round, with front-positioned eyes. These were not the same kind of creatures that had bit off poor George's fingers. But there were two of them, and they were staring at her. Something moved in the branches above her, rushing through the canopy. A fast shadow she barely caught, a sound more than an image.

When Sandra lowered her gaze, the blue lizard in front of her was a little closer. It stared at her, its long tail flailing this way and that. Like a cat studying a new toy. She was sure the little thing was actually smiling at her. She held its gaze, and it crouched again, like it was waiting. Slowly, very slowly, she bent down and picked up a fallen branch, gripping it as a weapon. She watched as the small lizard in front of her took a tentative step forward, took a branch too, and held it just like she was holding it. They faced each other, each one holding on to their weapon. It kept its eyes on her as it balanced on its hind legs.

Two more of the little lizards scuttled out of the bushes and stood there looking at Sandra.

She tried to boldly advance, hoping her movement would scare them off. The lizards jumped back and ran for about two yards, and then stopped to once again sit on their haunches, staring at her. They behaved like lemurs or prairie dogs she had seen in documentaries. She turned. There were two of them, now, following her.

"Get out of my way," she breathed.

The one that carried the branch popped up and down on its legs, and made a sound, chirping and twittering. Its companions replied with almost the identical sound.

"Listen, I'd like to stay here and play but I must go."

Again the one with the branch hopped up and down, while it gargled a long string of clicks and squeals and chirrups and clucks.

Sandra did a double take.

"This is absolutely crazy," she said, loud and clear.

The lizard chanted again its series of sounds, and at this point Sandra was sure: the sounds the thing was emitting followed the same rhythm, and the same intonation of her speech. The same pattern.

The little bugger was mocking her.

There was a sound from above, and Sandra looked up.

One of the creatures dropped on her with a screech, arms and legs outstretched.

Twenty years of weekly tennis games kicked in and Sandra intercepted it with her stick, sending it flying in the bushes. It landed with a crash and an enraged squeal.

The other lizards scattered, chirping and twittering furiously, and Sandra started running.

CHAPTER 16

The Rex growled as it slammed into another tree. Under a shower of leaves and detritus, Jack rolled between the roots and scampered away. The dinosaur was still too big for it to follow. It tried to squeeze between two tree-trunks but its head was too wide. His back against the bark of the tree, Jack took a deep breath and considered his options.

A large, gooey object dropped on his shoulder. He jumped, and pushed it away. It fell to the ground with a squashy sound, leaving a big oily stain on his jacket, and slowly crept away. There were more of the slug-like creatures slowly descending along the bark. With a grimace, Jack decided it was best if he kept moving. He could see through the trees where the Rex was pacing up and down, sniffing and emitting a weird, song-like sound.

He went in the opposite direction, casting cautious glances overhead, careful where he stepped.

#

Terri was lost. The reality of what had happened to Dylan had begun percolating in her mind, and she shivered with cold, her heart pounding in her chest. There was forest in every direction, a thin layer of mist blurring the details. Ferns grew as high as her shoulder, and the ground felt spongy under her feet. Animals moved under cover of the vegetation, calling to each other with a chorus of strange sounds.

She decided to keep the sun on her right, and march in that direction.

A low branch caressed her cheek, and she pushed it back, and then passed a hand over her face to clean it of the dew. Only then she realized she was crying.

#

In the end, they cornered Sandra and started throwing stones at her. She braced herself, her back against a tree, one arm protecting her face, the other waving the stick to keep them at a distance.

One of the blue lizards jumped at her from the left, biting hard on her leg. Sandra shouted and kicked it, and sent it rolling under a bush.

The teeth had penetrated her denim pants and scratched her leg. Another took its place, and tried to bite through her shoe. She hit it with her stick, braining it.

More rocks flew at her. She ducked and started moving again.

Two lizards dropped from the canopy above her. Sandra grabbed the one that landed on her right shoulder. It twisted in her hand, trying to bite her. She threw it away. The other was busy trying to sneak inside her shirt. She grabbed its tail and pulled it out, its claws leaving three fire streaks on her chest. She slammed it against a rock. Its bones cracked and it was still. Then she hit two others with her stick.

But they kept coming.

Sandra fumbled with her bag. It was there somewhere—she had seen it.

One of the things ran up to her. She found the flare. A red flare, the sort that gets used in car crashes, to mark off the wreck and alert drivers. The lizard bit deep in her calf. She staggered, backed against a rock. She shook her leg, but the creature only bit harder. Sandra shouted, tore the wrapper away from the flare with her teeth and slammed its bottom on her thigh, firing it up. Then she pressed it against the blue scales of the creature biting her leg.

The lizard let go and screeched, trying to run away. The smell of burnt meat stung her nostrils. She hit the beast hard with her stick and then slowly slid down, sitting on the ground, the stick in her right and the red flare in her left hand. The blue lizards kept at a safe distance, jumping up and down and chattering excitedly. One or two threw stones at her. Her leg bled heavily. She could see how the smell of blood increased their agitation. They would run up to her, cast their projectiles, and then hastily retreat, while the rest of the tribe cheered them on. They did not have a good aim, thankfully.

She brandished her flare, wondering how long it would last.

#

Terri almost fell down the hole.

She had been walking through the vegetation like a sleepwalker, concentrating on putting one foot in front of the other, trying to ignore the sounds of the jungle, staring straight ahead, the terror of being swallowed whole like Dylan numbing her mind. Then all of a sudden the ground fell away under her foot, and she grabbed a vine to keep her balance. A handful of dirt fell and splashed below her. The shock, the sudden pressure on her chest, the dream-like sensation of falling, injected some lucidity in her.

She balanced on the edge of a large circular pit in the ground, a barrel-like hole with vertical walls, maybe thirty yards across. The white rock was riddled with cracks and holes, and tufts of vegetation sprouted here and there, but mostly the walls were barren. She looked down. Maybe thirty feet below, the bottom of the pit was filled with water, a circular lake fed by dozens of tiny streams that ran down the sides of the depression.

Now that she paused, she could hear the continuous sound of dripping, and smell the cold, damp smell of a pond. A cenote, she thought. They had looked at the photos, on guidebooks and on the web, while they were planning their trip. In Yucatan, ancient sacred wells, where the Maya had sacrificed to their gods. Dylan had laughed and joked about going there to swim in the water.

Another thing they had missed that would never be again.

But this place below her was cold and dreary. A bird-like lizard nested on a thin ledge. It spread its emerald-green wings and fluttered along the wall, screeching. Something splashed in the water, a hint of something sleek and snakelike living at the bottom of the pit.

Her head swam, and she took a step back, afraid she might actually fall over the edge. Terri suddenly felt very tired. But she could not afford to stop. She had to go back to the plane and, she hoped, to her companions. With a sigh, she scanned the other side of the gap, and spotted a tree with two crooked branches, more or less along her intended path.

She fixed that as her point of reference, she started slowly walking around the pit.

#

The flare sputtered and died, smoke trickling from the mouth of the tube.

The blue lizards perked up, their heads moving as one, all eyes fixed on Sandra. She had patched up her leg, and now tried to push herself up, back against the rock surface, to try and confront them.

A shout sounded in the clearing. Both Sandra and the lizards turned, to stare at Steve Tanner, who came running, waving his arms and wielding two torches. Rosita ran behind him, trying to set fire to a third torch.

The lizards chattered among themselves and then scattered so fast that they seemed to never have been there. They left behind sticks and stones.

Sandra closed her eyes and let out a sigh of relief.

"Are you all right?" Rosita asked, kneeling by her side.

She nodded. "One of those beasts bit me," she said. "Two, really."

Rosita checked her leg. "The wound is clean," she said.

"I am a doctor," Sandra said tiredly. "I know."

Steve was building a small fire. "The humidity is so high, this stuff will never catch fire," he said.

"I'd be careful about that," Sandra said.

"Come again?"

"The little bastards are intelligent. One of them was imitating me. The sound of my voice. He picked up a branch when I did. And they threw stones at me."

She showed them the bruises on her arms. Steve whistled.

"So I wouldn't give them any ideas," she went on. "Or in a few hours we'll face a band of torch-wielding whatever they are called."

"They might be protoceratosauroids of some kind, given the shape of their head," Steve said. "Smart and aggressive."

"That's them."

"They were pretty small for being protos," he observed. "But considering the general phyletic trend..."

Rosita shook her head and sighed. "Can we save the lecture for later?"

"Of course," Steve said. He eyed the fire, which was producing more smoke than flames. "They probably have the smarts of a chimp," he added. He came closer and helped Sandra to her feet. Sandra tried to put her weight on the wounded leg. She grimaced, and then nodded. "I can make it."

She rummaged in her bag and came up with her pack of Camels. She lit up a cigarette.

"Talk about giving them ideas," Steve said. He checked the tracks of the beasts. "You want to kill them with cancer."

Sandra smiled tiredly while he stood and walked back to her.

"What happened to my brother?"

She stared at him. "We split when the Tyrannosaurs attacked us."

Rosita cursed. "Tyrannosaurs? Like, a number of them?"

"Three small ones, say twenty feet long. They coordinated their attack. So we split."

The man shook his head. "Tyrannosauroids," he said. "Or whatever. It's not like we can say for certain. How far from here?"

"About two miles," Sandra said, pointing. "Dylan and Terri were there too."

"George?"

She shook her head. "He's dead."

Rosita cursed. "This is going downhill fast," she said.

Steve nodded. He took a deep breath, looking around. The blue lizards were gone, the jungle still. The air smelled of smoke. There was a distant sound of thunder. Time to make haste.

"Fine," he said. "You go back to the plane, I'll go and get my brother and the kids."

"The fuck you do," Rosita said. "We help Sandra back, get Mike to come with us, get Barreto's gun, and we go and look for the others."

He stared at her. "He's my brother."

"I know that. But you are not going out there alone. You said this is a dangerous place, and we've already lost one of ours."

"Which is the reason why we can't lose two hours coming and going like this. You see Sandra back, then you and Mike come join me. But I need to start now."

CHAPTER 17

Jack stood on the crest of a ridge and looked around. The Rex had given up on him, or was waiting for a few friends, or maybe it would pop up from somewhere soon. Couldn't be certain. But Jack had learned as a young man to take things as they were, without great expectations, and therefore he was ready for anything and expected nothing.

As far as the eye could see, the ground was a series of cracks and ridges that made the going like an obstacle race. The area reminded him of certain broken terrains in areas where an earthquake had hit. The ground was fragmented in tilted blocks, and he felt like an ant in a box of Legos. The trees were stilted, weak and crooked, and widely spaced, the grass grew in thick clumps, long blades an unhealthy yellow-green color, like the succulent plants his mother had kept in vases on the terrace of their home.

There were big bugs buzzing in the air, fluttering on frantic wings, and the sky stretched unimpeded, blue and without clouds.

Suddenly, two black shapes crossed the sky, the thunder of their rotors causing a cloud of birds, or more likely flying lizards, to take off in panic.

Jack watched the two big choppers as they cruised low over the top of the trees, and banked in a tight turn, pointing in the direction of the crash site.

"Yeah!"

He jumped and waved his arms, but he doubted the people on board saw him.

Then he stopped, reflecting.

Two civilian choppers, very large. No Venezuelan Air Force, no sky ambulances. Yet very aggressive looking for civilian aircraft. With open side doors, gunship style. Cruising very fast and low over the jungle.

He bit the corner of his mouth.

This was like Apocalypse fucking Now, with only Wagner missing.

What the hell was happening?

Then he heard a woman screaming.

#

The hum of the rotors caused them to stop talking and look up.

"Helicopter!"

"Two of them," Rosita said.

Through the network of branches and leaves they barely saw the dark shapes of two large aircraft as they sped across the sky.

Rosita was quick in removing the red stop from the parachute rocket.

"A forest fire is the last thing we need," Steve said.

"Have a little faith," she smirked, pulling the cord. The rocket punched through the canopy and arched through the sky, blazing red.

Rosita discarded the spent tube.

"They are homing on our beacon," she said. "We should find a way to get in touch with the camp. They could help us search for the others."

Steve glanced at her.

"Jack can take care of himself," she said. "We can't get scattered through this shitty jungle, not any more than we are already."

"He's my brother," he said again.

Rosita could feel his anguish and was surprised at how much it pained her. "I know." She stopped, her arms akimbo. "Now listen to me. You are a scientist. Let's talk chances. Statistics. What gives us a better odd of really helping Jack and the kids? Rambling about? Or we take one hour off, but then come back with more people, radios, the works?"

Steve grimaced.

Sandra looked from Steve to Rosita. "I can make it on my own," she said. "You two go and get the others."

Rosita snorted. "I'm not leaving you alone and wounded in this jungle."

"It's just a scratch, and there's little choice, don't you think?"

They stared each other in the eye. "I—"

Sandra smirked. "I know. I'll be all right."

She took a water bottle from her first aid bag, and then handed the bag to Rosita. Then she turned to Steve. "You get Jack and the kids back, okay? And take care of this little lady."

Then she picked up her stick and walked away, leaving behind a trail of smoke, following the faint track Steve and Rosita had opened in the undergrowth.

They watched her go, limping.

"What was that about?" Steve asked.

"Get going," Rosita replied. "The guys could be in trouble."

#

Trees and bushes in every direction, deep shadows over which a thin mist hung.

"Yo! There!"

Jack looked around.

"Here! Help!"

He tried to pinpoint the direction of the call.

He waded through the foliage. "Keep talking!"

"I'm here! Help me!"

Finally, he almost stumbled upon Terri. She was shoulder-deep in a pool of what could only possibly be quicksand.

"Hold still!"

He chose a branch from a nearby tree. He grabbed it in both hands and pulled, loading all of his weight into it. The wood flexed and creaked, and finally gave with a loud snap. He quickly cleaned it of the excess leaves.

"Don't worry," he said. Keep talking and distract her, he thought. Panic is bad. "We've seen this in lots of movies, right? It's gonna be all right."

She lifted her head. "Only movie I remember, the guy died."

Jack clicked his tongue. "Poor taste in movies."

Then, stepping carefully, he got close to the quicksand patch and stretched, pushing the branch almost in Terri's face. She struggled with the sand, and finally reached out with a hand, grabbing the end of the offshoot.

"Hold on tight."

Terri was a slip of a girl, but Jack had to put in a lot of effort to drag her out of the soup. He dug his heels into the ground and took care to pull with his whole body, using both arms and legs. The girl lifted her other arm and took a firmer hold on the wood. Jack gritted his teeth and pulled again, and with a gelatinous sucking sound, the quicksand pit released its prisoner.

Terri remained prone on the ground for a moment, her T-shirt and jeans gray and caked with mud, her hair disheveled.

"See? You gotta watch the right movies."

"Thank you," she gasped.

Around them, the sounds of the jungle resumed, uncertainly at first, then with habitual enthusiasm.

"Where's Dylan?" he asked finally.

Terri stared at him. Then she burst out crying.

PART III

CHAPTER 18

The voice of the pilot came muffled through the headphones.

"Fucking jungle."

Schneider grunted in agreement. From the vantage point of the second pilot's seat, the top of the plateau appeared like a solid green surface, rippling in the breeze, a tall palm tree sticking out here and there. Birds rose in panic as the two helicopters moved toward the constant pinging of the electronic tracking device.

"Last thing I want is to suck a fucking pigeon through the intakes," the pilot grunted.

"They are staying out of the way."

"Smart pigeons. Look at that."

There was a lane, cut through the jungle like a landing strip. The traces of a plane's emergency landing were unmistakable, about twenty yards wide and over a quarter of a mile long, running along a low, rocky crest. Deep grooves dug in the grassland, exposing the dirt beneath. A fallen tree.

"Ten hours."

Schneider leaned forward and saw the tail of the Pilatus, upturned like a strange tower.

The radio crackled.

"Did you see that?"

The pilot grunted. "Bravo 2, this is Bravo 1, please repeat."

"Bravo 1, Bravo 2 here, did you spot the big bird at five hours?"

Schneider turned and scanned the horizon. "I can't see anything," he said.

"It was a flash, boss, but it was big. Some kind of eagle or condor."

"Take a shot for Wildlife the next time it shows up," Schneider said. "Now let's stick to the plan. Over."

"Bravo 2, copy that."

Schneider grimaced. Tight schedules meant picking less-than-professional assets.

"At three hours, boss."

He looked down. There was the relic of the Pilatus, a dented white metal cylinder, laying on its side, wings broken. It lay against the rocks.

People.

Schneider looked at the three figures. Two men and a woman in a red dress.

"Let's take a tour and then put us down."

The pilot acknowledged and clicked his radio. "Bravo 2, we are going down."

"Roger, Bravo 1, we'll watch over you."

#

"That's a Hip," Mike said.

"A what?" Maria Barreto asked.

"It's the NATO name. Mil-MI-17. A Russian transport chopper." Mike was shaking his head. "There's something off."

"Why?"

He grimaced. "No identification signs."

The big camo-pattern helicopter hovered about one hundred feet over the stretch of jungle that the Pilatus had cleared in its landing. The light played with the rotors, giving it a trembling halo. The drone of the engine was not as loud as Mike would have expected.

"That's a chartered chopper. No Venezuelan air force, no Brazilians, no air rescue."

"You said you did not care for who would come and rescue us," Hernan Barreto said.

"Up to a point, kid. Up to a point," Mike said.

"Maybe they asked some private company for support," Maria said. But she sounded uncertain, too.

Just then, a second helicopter appeared, identical to the first, hovering at about twice the height of the first.

A covering station. Like they expected trouble. Like the second chopper was ready to gun down any attackers on the ground. Like they knew there were dangerous beasts here. Which would be strange, and suspect. "This is not good," Mike said. "Wait here."

While the other two gathered in front of the wreck, waving their arms and calling, he slipped back inside.

#

Crouching behind a bush, Sandra felt a shiver run down her spine when the first chopper landed and a dozen men in fatigues climbed down. They carried weapons. The second machine kept flying, in an obvious covering position.

Fear crushed her guts. Whatever was going on, this was no rescue mission. She had spent too much time in dark corners of the world not to recognize the types. Their clothes, their movements, their weapons. The way they fanned out on the ground, the way they looked around, arms at the ready. These were mercenaries, or professional soldiers of some kind.

She saw Hernan Barreto walk towards the men, his wife two steps behind. *Where was Mike?*

Hernan stopped and the leader of the rescuers came forward. He was not wearing any special signs, but it was obvious he was in charge. Tall, broad-shouldered, he was the only one not wearing a cap, his short blond hair contrasting with his ruddy complexion.

They were speaking, the men on the lookout. Scanning the trees, checking out the plane.

Sandra turned to the plane, too. It took her a moment to realize that the wreck had changed position. Then she saw Mike sneaking behind the fuselage, out of sight of the armed men. She squinted, trying to figure out what was going on.

That was when a gunshot echoed in the silence.

#

"Mister Barreto." Schneider smiled.

Hernan smiled back. Maria had been right: his father had sent his men to rescue him.

"It's a pleasure seeing you, Mister Schneider," he said.

Schneider nodded, then lifted his eyes and nodded a greeting to Maria. "Mrs. Barreto."

Hernan eyed the rest of the company. Two men stood by the chopper, while the other six had opened up in a fan formation. They carried Kalashnikovs and wore unmarked fatigues.

"You mounted a big operation," he said.

"I don't like taking chances, Mister Barreto. Nor does your father."

"I was sure the old man—"

"There's other people," Maria said, behind him.

Hernan wondered why she had not come closer.

"Yes, Mrs. Barreto. We have a list of passengers."

"Is this the reason why you brought two helicopters?"

Schneider looked at her, his eyes two ice-blue slits. "Standard procedure," he said.

"You must excuse my wife." Hernan grinned, barely glancing back at her. "She's been under much stress. It's been a taxing experience for everyone, as you can imagine."

Schneider nodded. "Now there's nothing to worry about anymore."

Hernan turned, looking at the battered, dented wreck of the Pilatus. Where the hell was the pilot?

"I guess you could give us a lift," he said, turning. "And let your men take care of the rest of them. I'm dying for a shower." He lifted his bandaged, splinted arm. "And I'll need to see a doctor."

There was a long moment of silence.

Schneider snapped his fingers. Two of his men, a big scarred brute and a leering guy that kept staring at Maria, stepped forward.

Before Hernan could understand what was happening, Schneider had barked an order.

He turned to see his wife run, her long legs pumping. The scarred man lifted his weapon and fired a single shot.

"What—!"

Maria stumbled forward and dove into the thick of the vegetation.

"Go get her!" Schneider snapped.

"What is happening here?" Hernan asked. His voice broke, authority crumbling and leaving the field to fear.

"You don't need to worry, Mister Barreto." Schneider grinned. "We are here to take care of the mess you made."

#

Sandra imagined more than saw Maria sprint towards the jungle, and the man in camo lift his rifle. The gunshot was already a memory and the young woman in red was jumping into the bushes. Sandra turned. Barreto still stood by the mercenary leader. She saw Mike run to the jungle in turn, the crushed hull of the plane giving him cover but for the last few meters.

Shouts saluted his appearance. Mike crouched lower and kept running, and before anyone could do anything, the jungle closed over him.

Limping and squatting, Sandra moved to the place where Maria had entered the trees.

Two men were coming toward her, moving fast, guns ready. Sandra looked around. There was blood smeared on the bark of a tree. A hand touched her shoulders and she jumped, a hand stopping her mouth, stifling her cry.

"It's me!"

Mike let her go. The men in camo were a few meters away.

The pilot lifted a gun. Barreto's, Sandra realized.

Then the foliage exploded, and a giant lizard stomped into the clearing.

People started screaming.

#

There was automatic fire rattling behind them as they ran through the trees. Mike was holding her up, an arm encircling her waist.

"What was that?"

"A Tyrannosaurus," Sandra said.

"Shit!"

The gunfire stopped, the roars and the screams of the monster suddenly silent.

They turned, slowing down. "I guess a bunch of trigger-happy mofos was more than enough for it," Mike said.

"There could be more around," Sandra said. "They hunt in packs."

"No kidding."

They hastened, Mike opening the way, helping Sandra along. "What happened to your leg?"

"Long story. George is dead, we scattered. Steve and Rosy are going to try and get the others together."

Mike cursed.

"Who are those guys anyway?"

Mike grunted. "Friends of Barreto's."

"But not of his wife."

He pointed. "We might ask her."

Maria Barreto lay crumpled at the foot of a large tree, her red dress impossible to miss. Sandra sat down by her side and checked her pulse.

There was a large wound in the woman's side. Sandra went instinctively for her bag, only to remember she no longer had it. With a grimace, she ripped the hem of Maria's gown, and used it to stop the bleeding.

"I always saw that in movies," Mike said.

"Me too, and I always thought it extremely stupid."

They gently turned the unconscious girl. "The bullet went clean through."

Mike looked around. He noticed a large beetle-like insect crawling around the tree trunk, antennae waving. "We can't stay here."

Sandra looked at him. "I can stop the bleeding. Can you carry her?"

He just nodded. The woman went to work, ripping more strips from the red dress.

CHAPTER 19

Schneider kicked the still body of the big lizard.

"This is unexpected," he said.

The men behind him traded a glance. They had discharged their Kalashnikovs at it, and still the thing had come at them, its big jaws agape.

"Hard to kill bastard," Mick said.

"The plateau is—" Barreto shook his head. "There's dozens of the things. One of the guys said this is some sort of island ecology or something."

Schneider did not turn. He kept staring into the open eyes of the monster. "Are they all this big?"

"Some are bigger. There was a herd here, early this morning."

Hernan pointed at the dented hull of the crashed plane. "One of them pushed the plane from there," he indicated, "to where it sits now."

"Indeed."

Ortega and Mick came back. "The girl's gone in deep, but she's wounded," Mick said.

"And the man?"

Mick shrugged. "There's a clear path where he moved. It's not like they'll be hard to trace."

"Fine, set up search parties and start combing the jungle." Schneider kicked the dead dinosaur again. "And keep your eyes open."

"Will do."

Ortega hesitated. "Is this Plan B, boss?"

Schneider smirked. "Something like that, yes."

While the men regrouped, he detached the radio from his belt. "Your father was worried about you," he said to Hernan.

Barreto smiled. Schneider gave instructions for the second carrier to land. Rounding up the survivors would be more complicated than planned.

Pragmatic at heart, he had already taken the presence of dinosaurs in his stride. He did not care for mysteries, extinct animals, and weirdness. They were just a complication. A further problem to be taken care of.

Hernan Barreto hovered by his side, smiling like a big, stupid puppy. Schneider decided he would take care of him personally. It would be good to wipe the smartass grin from Hernan's bronzed face.

He looked at the sky. Dark clouds gathered.

#

"I'm just saying this is weird as hell," Ortega said.

"You think it's PsyOps?"

They had made a stop to try and make sense of the situation. Above the cover of intertwined branches, the dark clouds rumbled with thunder, promising a free shower for everyone in a few minutes. The jungle was thick and forbidding.

"You think they dosed us on LSD or some other X-files shit?" Tim said.

He took his canteen out and took a sip of water. Then stopped and looked suspiciously at the water bottle.

"I dunno," Ortega said. "But you saw that big motherfucker back there. Now don't you tell me that's normal, 'cos it ain't."

"Some experiment, like in the Jurassic shit movie?" Tim offered.

"There's still lots of blank spaces on the map." Mick shrugged.

"Yeah." Tim laughed. "Ever told you about that time I was chartered to hunt the Loch Ness Monster?"

"By the way, did you see the way the boss reacted?" Mick asked. "Damn, he really creeped me out."

Tim glanced at him. "Why?"

"A cool boss is a fine thing, but too cool a boss can be trouble."

"You don't know what you are talking about," Ortega said over his shoulder. "The boss pulled me out of some tight spots you can't even imagine. He's made of steel, and wired with ice, and that's what you need in a tight corner. So be respectful."

"You were with him on the Angola-Namibian border?"

"And other places too."

Mick stopped. "Is it true? What they say he did in Cunene?"

"We don't discuss this sort of thing," Ortega replied.

Tim laughed. "What happens in Cunene stays in Cunene."

Ortega told him to fuck off, and fired up his com-link.

"This is Tango 1."

He listened for a moment, nodding. "Yeah, looks like the chick got some support. She's bleeding, but now there's other people with her. Two, maybe three."

He gazed at Tim and Mick, arching his eyebrows. "Yeah, Roger to that."

Thunder grumbled over them.

"Gentlemen," he said, "let's move our asses."

Mick and Tim cursed.

"Look on the bright side, guys. This salad's so thick, we won't even get wet."

"Not from the rain. But I'm sweating like a pig already."

"Tell me something new, Mick."

#

"We are going in the wrong direction," Rosita said.

"I know," Steve answered. "But it's not like we can vault over that crack hanging from vines. I'm no Tarzan, and you're no Jane."

They stopped, taking a breath. She looked around. "How come we always end up in this place?" she asked.

They were about twenty yards from the place where the creek poured off the plateau in a sparkling cascade.

"It's not like this is a big place," he said.

"I bet you bring all your dates here."

He smiled.

Rosita placed a hand on his arm. "Jack is fine," she said. "You boys are survivors, right?"

He patted her hand. "I'm the older brother. I am responsible."

"I know. I have two brothers."

"Okay, sweethearts, hands up and nobody gets hurt."

Steve and Rosita turned and stared at the two men.

Both men wore camo fatigues and carried what to Steve looked like Kalashnikovs. They wore com headphones and looked a little too old and mean to be Venezuelan or Brazilian army. They had their guns at the ready and were not doing anything to look reassuring. Something was definitively off.

"Hands up you two!" one of them repeated.

"What the hell?" Rosita stared. "We are the ones you are supposed to rescue!"

"That's for us to decide, babe."

Rosita scowled. "Babe?"

One of the guys walked into the stream. He waved his gun, motioning for them to hold their hands up.

"I think there's part of this story that we've not been told," Steve said.

"Shut up!"

The other man spoke into his radio. "This is Tango 3, we've got two of them."

He glanced at them, and shook his head. "No. Big guy, small Chink chick. Roger."

"What's this sound?" his companion asked.

The guy on the radio listened. "People?"

Both Steve and Rosita exchanged a glance. They knew the sound all right. The continuous chattering of the theropods was drifting from the distance.

"Tango 3, we have contact. More people incoming."

"That's not people," Steve said.

The other guy signaled him to stand back. "What is it then?"

"It's animals, potentially dangerous animals."

"Dinosaurs," Rosita said.

The man with the gun laughed. The sound of the theropod flock was coming closer, and now they could also hear the snapping of branches and the rustling of the foliage.

"We need to get away from here," Steve said, lowering his voice. "Now!"

"We don't go anywhere until we get orders."

The first shapes emerged from the undergrowth, a column of rust-colored, long-necked lizards. One of the men cursed. The other just laughed and took two steps toward the animals, his feet splashing in the shallow water of the stream.

"What in the fuck—"

"We need to move," Steve said again, with urgency, his voice as soft as possible. He lowered his hands, and one of the two men pointed his assault rifle at him.

"Hold!" he barked.

Tanner's eyes widened. "That's not a good idea," he whispered.

The flock of theropods stopped cold.

"What does it mean?" the second man asked, his voice echoing in the clearing.

"Shut the fuck up!" Rosita hissed.

"You shut the fuck up, woman!" the man replied, loud and clear, waving his gun. The animals turned as one, dozens of heads moving like weather vanes in the wind, unblinking yellow eyes and sharp white teeth. Some tilted their heads on one side or another, others stretched their necks to get a better view, but apart from that, the coelophysis were perfectly still. And all were looking in their direction.

Rosita cursed under her breath and looked around. Too little time to try and climb a tree. The stream cut a deep notch in the lip of the cliff, and the trees there parted to show them a stretch of blue sky, a vast expanse of clouds, and to the foreground, a sea of waving treetops.

She slowly lowered her hands. The men in camo were too intent on staring at the dinosaurs to notice. Tanner did the same, glancing at her.

He gave a little interrogative shrug. She nodded, and took a deep breath. She cast a final glance at the clouds and the trees, she listened to the echo of the waterfall.

"Jump!" she shouted.

"What?"

She grasped him by the wrist and they ran to the edge of the cliff. One of the men cried out and turned, bullets slamming into the vegetation.

The dinosaurs let out a high chirp and moved as one, a screeching mass of sharp-teethed horrors. Screaming at the top of her lungs, Rosita dragged Steve along, splashing in the low water of the creek, keeping low. When they reached the very edge of the clearing, they jumped together.

For an eternity, they were suspended in the air. Behind them, the rattling of the guns gave way to the screams of the men and the sound of the dinosaurs' feeding frenzy.

Then they crashed through the canopy of the forest below, and tumbled down, branches and vines breaking their fall, slapping their faces, ripping their clothes, until they crashed into the ice-cold water of a deep lake.

CHAPTER 20

Schneider was not pleased. While gorging himself on a meal-pack, Hernan Barreto had explained that his wife, Maria, was carrying a copy of the documents on her person.

"The cross," Hernan said around a mouthful. He pointed at his own chest. "It's a USB thumb drive."

Schneider closed his eyes. And of course Maria Barreto was bleeding to death somewhere in a dinosaur-infested jungle. He opened his eyes again and smiled at Barreto. Then he turned and walked away from the Hip.

"Problems, boss?" one of the men asked.

Marais, he remembered. French, former Legion. Communications.

"Patch me with all the field teams," Schneider said.

The man hastened to comply. He handed Schneider the microphone.

"This is Tango Leader. Looks like we are going for Plan B after all. We absolutely must find the woman in the red dress. Our main concern will be finding her. All other crash survivors are no-priority. Please check back and confirm."

"This is Tango 1," Ortega's voice crackled through the airwaves. "Roger that. No-priority as in free targeting practice?"

Schneider considered. He had no obligations towards the other passengers, but why waste resources?

"No. Bring them here, but don't worry should they be damaged along the way."

Ortega clicked his com to acknowledge.

"This is Tango 2, I read you boss."

"Tango 4 copy, boss."

Then silence. Schneider and Marais looked at each other.

The transmission fizzed, then a voice came back online. "Tango 3, copy and confirm. Gallo, are you out there? Talk to me, man."

"What about Tango 3?" Schneider asked.

"They were on about fifteen minutes ago, had two passengers. A big guy and a Chink."

"The second pilot and probably one of the Tanners." Schneider nodded. "Call them again."

"Yes boss."

Then Marais turned. "But I would not be worried," he said. "Communications are a bitch in this place."

"I'm not worried," Schneider replied. "Gallo is a professional. But you keep calling them."

"Of course."

He looked back at the chopper. Hernan was sitting inside, finishing his vanilla fudge. The young man grinned and gave Schneider a thumbs-up.

#

They staggered out of the lake, soaking wet and out of breath. Rosita let out a loud, yodeling shout.

"You could have killed us both!" Tanner told her. His voice echoed against the rock face, louder than the thunder of the waterfall.

"You said there was a lake down here," she said.

"What?"

"The other day, when we were exploring. You said there was a lake at the foot of the waterfall."

He stared at her, incredulous. "And based on that—?"

She stared at him, open-mouthed. "You weren't sure?" she asked back, her eyes flaring. "You were bullshitting me all along?"

She stepped up to him and punched him right in the face. "You fucking bastard, we could have broken our necks!"

She followed up with a series of blows to the body, Steve trying to cover his face and parry her fists with his arms. "I just said that given the sound and the calcareous nature of the mother rock—"

"Mother rock, my ass! You said there was a fucking lake and I fucking believed you!"

Steve took two limping steps to the side, still trying to avoid her blows. His trouser leg was stained red.

"Wait, you hurt?"

He stared at her. "Afraid a wound might kill me before you do?"

She cursed and pushed him against a tree trunk. She knelt down to check his blood-soaked trouser leg. "Of all the stupid macho things," she mumbled.

"Look who's talking."

She ripped open the trouser and grimaced at the blood. She used a piece of the ripped cloth to clean the wound, making a show of ignoring his wail. He offered her his water bottle, and she poured some water over the raw flesh.

"It won't kill you," she said.

A bullet had dug a two-inch-long groove along the calf.

"We need to wrap the thing up tight and you'll be as good as new," she said, standing up and cleaning her hands on her back pockets.

"So you can start punching me again?"

Her eyes flared again. "You damn idiot, do you have any idea of what—?"

"But then, there was a lake," he grinned.

Rosita just snorted and started rummaging in the bag for some bandages.

"Have you noticed?" he said.

"What?"

She crushed the roll of gauze to dry it.

"No gunshots, no screams."

Eyes closed, Rosita remained in silence for a minute, listening. "Jesus," she said. "It's already over?"

He sat down on the ground, squeezing water from the hem of his shirt. "As I said, this is not our world."

Rosita finished bandaging his leg. "One would think machine guns make a difference."

"Oh, they do make a difference, if you know what to expect and don't panic."

"This place is a fucking death trap."

She sat down by his side. They were in a pool of sunlight, a pillar of sunshine penetrating through the canopy and painting a rainbow above the lake. Their clothes were drying fast. He glanced at her and put an arm around her shoulders. She didn't punch him in the face, so he imagined it was all right.

They sat like that for some time, resting.

"Who are those men?" Rosita asked. "Surely not some kind of rescue team."

"They were looking for someone, and there's more of them."

"This has something to do with Barreto," she said.

"You hate that guy!"

"Rich daddy's boy that slaps his wife around and packs a gun. Need anything else?"

Steve thought about it. "It might be political. They may be here for Sandra."

"They send in Rambo for a doctor?"

"She works for Emergency. Emergency gets a lot of political flak, and our doctor is a pretty outspoken lady."

Rosita gave a nod. "Yeah, I heard her screech in her telephone, back in Fonte Boa. She was chewing some poor guy's head off."

Then she shook her head. "You want her dead, you hear her plane crashed, and send in the 7th Airborne to make sure she's dead?"

They were silent for a while. Rosita looked up. The sun painted splotches of light over the white face of the cliff, the yellow beams made solid by the mist hanging in the air. Bird calls echoed over the roar of the waterfall.

Only they were not birds, she reminded herself.

"Birds fly," she said.

"So they tell me."

She dug her elbow in his ribs. "What I mean is, you said there's no birds up here, because the dinos are the birds, right?"

"More or less, yes."

"But birds fly. How come no bird flew up here and sort of established a foothold?"

He closed his eyes and ran a hand through his wet hair. "Remember the bit about this being their very own box? It's just like that. This place is fine-tuned for dinos, exactly as the jungle down there is fine tuned for recent floras and faunas. Trespassers are not equipped to survive. Which also explains why there's no dinos, flying or otherwise, down there. Those that tried to move in, ended up dead before they could reproduce."

"Shit. It will happen to us too, won't it?"

"What? Dying before we can reproduce?"

She snorted. "Very funny. This place is a death trap," she repeated.

"The wonders of natural selection, baby."

"Don't you baby me, you fat man!"

She stood and offered him her hand, helping him up. "Let's find a way to get back over there," she said.

Steve took a pair of tentative steps, and nodded. "I can make it."

"Good boy!"

They started south, following the rock face.

"You know," she said. "I think I can pilot one of those twirly birds."

CHAPTER 21

Ortega raised a fist and team Tango 1 stopped. They were in an area with moderate visibility, the trees far between and the ferns waist-high.

Ortega tapped his left ear with two fingers. Tim and Mick could hear it too. A woman's voice, talking excitedly. Mick grinned and shook his head. One thing you always could count on: chicks always talked. Ortega waved and they spread, moving slowly, careful about making noise. Ortega took point, Tim and Mick as wings. Then they advanced, closing in on the woman and her companions.

The voice stopped. The men did likewise.

The forest was uncannily silent for two long minutes. Then the voice started again.

Ortega could not make the words scan. But he recognized the rhythm of speech, the feminine intonation, the tone rising and falling.

Tatatata-ta. Tata. Ta. Ta.

The trees opened and they were on the edge of a large clearing, blue-green ferns waving gently. One of those ubiquitous chunks of gray rock sat in the center of the clearing. The voice came from behind it. Ortega checked his men's position, and then pointed for them to spread further, covering the whole space.

Then he advanced into the open.

"Come out slowly, miss," he said, his voice loud and clear. "We don't want to hurt you. We're friends. We don't want to hurt anybody."

The chattering stopped, and then something uncanny happened. A man's voice sounded from behind the rock. With the corner of his eye Ortega caught Tim standing up, mouth open.

The man's voice repeated whatever it had said before. It sounded a lot like Ortega.

Tim took a step forward. Ortega cursed him for a fool.

"Come out of there!" he barked. "Now!"

The voice was silent for a moment. Then it said something that sounded a lot like "Kowowaehee. Kow!"

"It's a fucking parrot!" Tim said.

A flash of movement, and there on the gray rook stood a small lizard, dark blue and orange. It balanced on its hind legs, staring at Ortega with bright yellow eyes. It chirruped, and then it repeated its imitation trick, letting out a long sequence of sounds that weren't words but sounded a lot like human speech.

"Well, bugger me!" Ortega said.

The lizard stared at him, tilted its head this way and that, and then repeated it almost perfectly.

Tim and Mick moved closer, laughing.

"Shit, man, the critter got you down quite right," Tim said.

There was rustling in the ferns.

Mick turned sharply, weapon ready. "What--?"

The blue lizard was gone. A distant cry of "Bugger me!" made them turn to their right. Then two blue lizards jumped Tim. The man screamed as one of the creatures bit into his hand and the other went for his face. He grabbed the blue lizard by the neck and pulled it away just as three others shot out of the greenery and landed on his back and shoulders.

"Get them off me!"

Ortega was the quickest to react. He let go of the gun and pulled out his combat knife. One of the blue lizards bit him in the calf. He kicked it away, ignoring the pain. Mick was shooting blindly into the ferns, which were regurgitating a horde of the little buggers. Tim went down screaming.

"Stop it!" Ortega shouted, fending another attacker off with his knife.

But Mick had obviously lost it. When his AK-74 clicked on empty, he ejected the magazine and slapped another in the gun, pulling the lever. It took him maybe ten seconds, time enough for a handful of the monsters to attack him. One climbed on his chest, tail whipping. Others grabbed his arms and legs, biting, screeching. Mick dropped his gun and fumbled for his knife.

Ortega killed another of the creatures and stomped on one that was trying to bite through his boot. "Let's get out!"

Mick let out an incoherent cry. One of the things was dangling from his shoulder, its jaws firmly closed on his flesh at the base of the man's neck. Others bit his arms and his legs.

Then a bang echoed in the clearing.

Ortega knifed another beast and turned. One of the blue lizards was trying to pick up Mick's fallen weapon. It braced the stock on the ground for leverage, and pulled it up, grabbing the body of the AK.

"Oh, shit!"

Its tiny hand grasped the trigger and the weapon started firing, rocking and turning on itself and dragging the creature along in its dance. Ortega cursed and hit the dirt, ignoring the blue creatures surrounding him as a shower of bullets zinged through the air, cutting through the ferns and hitting the trees in a shower of bark splinters. One bullet hit Mick in the belly. It was a carnival of bullets and noise, and it lasted a few seconds.

When the gun was finally silent, the lizards were gone. Ortega stood, limping and bleeding from a dozen wounds. He clicked the radio, panting, but got only static. He cast a quick glance at the bloody ruin that was Tim, prodded Mick with the tip of his boot, and then ran back in the direction of the chopper like Hell itself was on his heels.

Thunder rolled above, and a thick rain started falling.

CHAPTER 22

The forest ended abruptly, a sharp straight line in the landscape, the rest of the plateau a vast grassy prairie.

"You sure this is the right way?" Rosita asked.

Steve sighed. "Look," he said. He spread his arms, facing the white cliff. "There's a fault running like this. It cuts the plateau and caused this side to slide down. Or the other side to lift up."

He placed his hands together, flat in front of him, palms down. "This block did not just drop, it also tilted, like this." He mimed the movement. "Like a pair of scissors. So, going that way, we'll find a lower escarpment. Because the face of the cliff is a triangle, and it closes to the north."

Rosita looked at him and arched an eyebrow. "Are you sure of this?"

He dropped his head. "Yes."

"Like you were about the lake?"

"Again?"

She chuckled, and he turned his back to her, starting slowly north. "I'd wish you found a better subject for flirting."

"For—?" Rosita sprinted after him. "You big oaf!"

Thunder boomed above them.

#

"This place is weird."

Jack turned and stared at Terri. These were her first words in an hour. And she was right, the place was weird.

It was as if somebody had cleared a round area of forest, an almost perfect circle, twenty yards across. The ground was covered with short grass, and there were no trees and no bushes. Only the branches of the tallest trees surrounding the space stretched over it, intertwining in a sort of high ceiling, through which sunlight penetrated in solid-looking shafts. Hot and humid, a greenish haze hung in the air.

"Looks like the High Court of the Elves," the girl said.

Jack cleared his throat.

She turned to him. "I'm just saying." She gave him a mirthless smile. "I'm not losing my mind or something. Just this place looks so—"

"Uncanny."

"Fantasy," she said.

They took a few steps forward, then stopped suddenly. In front of them, in a depression about two yards across, twenty-four football-sized eggs rested in a neat circle.

"A nest."

There were more all around.

A dozen precisely spaced nests, each one a barren, compressed dirt depression, held a score of smooth, dark gray eggs.

"This is some sort of incubator," Jack said. "Or coop."

"You mean somebody built it? Like, people?"

He shook his head. "No. They did it. The dinos. One of the breeds of dinosaurs. I think it's called a nesting ground."

"Judging by the eggs, they must be large ones."

"We better get out of here. Fast."

There was a loud honking sound, coming from the margin of the clearing.

"Shit!"

A large creature, like a ten-feet tall duck-billed kangaroo, walked into the nesting ground. It stared at them.

"Mommy's home," Jack whispered, pushing Terri behind. He gripped his folding spade in both hands. The duck-billed dinosaur opened its mouth and bellowed a frightful, thundering call. It started roosting with its left foot.

"When I tell you, run," Jack said.

"But—"

"Run!"

The creature roared and charged them.

Jack rolled on the ground and swung his spade, trying to hit the duck-billed monster in the head. It snapped back, avoiding contact, and then lunged forward again, snarling.

Jack jumped back. The monster's teeth closed on the blade of the spade. It ripped it from Jack's fingers and then spat it away.

He looked around. Terri stood at the edge of the clearing, staring at the confrontation.

Stupid girl.

"Run!" he shouted.

Then he waved his arms, moving sideways, trying to maintain distance and get close to the spot where his tool had landed. The dinosaur stared at him, studying his movements.

"Hey!"

Jack risked a glance.

Terri was standing in the middle of one of the nests, holding two eggs, one in each hand. "These are what it's all about, right?"

The duck-headed dinosaur turned toward the young woman and froze.

Cautiously, Jack moved to pick his spade up again.

"I don't think that's a good idea," he said, without raising his voice.

The dinosaur ignored him.

Jack ran his hands on his sides, and his fingers brushed against the tube of the parachute rocket in his pocket. He pulled it out and started unscrewing the red cap at the bottom.

Terri crouched and placed one of the eggs on the ground. Very gently, she rolled it to the edge of the depression. It collided with another egg and stopped.

Jack reached the shadows of the trees. A stomping sound, then another. There were other duck-billed dinosaurs coming. He saw them approach from the other side of the clearing, attracted by the noise, maybe by their smell. At the center of the clearing, Terri was still engaged in her staring contest with her dino.

Jack pointed the rocket tube at the newcomers and gave the string a hard pull. There was a low *bop* and the mouth of the tube belched out a cloud of smoke, and then a bright red fireball flew towards the two duck billed monsters, a miniature red sun following a very erratic path.

The creatures emitted a high call and scrambled away, crashing through the jungle.

Jack started moving swiftly to reach Terri, just as the dinosaur sprinted toward the young woman.

Jack screamed. Terri screamed. A loud bang sounded in the clearing, and the dinosaur stumbled, half turned, and crashed on the ground, crushing its dead weight onto the contents of one of the nests.

Three men emerged from the trees. They wore camo suits and carried big guns. Terri stared at them. Jack closed his eyes and leaned against the bark of the closest tree. The rescuers had come.

Terri's scream opened his eyes. He crouched down in the undergrowth and watched as one of the men grabbed Terri by the wrist, shaking her, while one of his companions covered the clearing and the third, a high power rifle carried casually on his shoulder, examined his prey.

A second duck-headed dinosaur came into the clearing. The guy with the long-barreled power rifle shouted something, embraced his gun and fired. The second dinosaur staggered and fell. Just like that.

"Now," the guy at the center of the clearing shouted, "are you coming out with your hands up high, or should we start firing into the bushes?"

And without waiting for a response, he let open with his assault rifle, peppering the bushes with bullets.

"Hold it, hold it!"

Jack stood, keeping his hands in plain view.

"See," the one that held Terri leered. "You can catch more flies with sugar than with vinegar."

Jack stared at them.

"You are the strangest rescue team I ever saw," he said.

"Shut the fuck up, baldy," the one with the long rifle said. He turned to the assault rifle guy. "Tell the boss we have two of them."

Thunder sounded overhead. Long Rifle waved his gun at Jack, motioning him towards Terri. "Let's beat it, before we get a shower."

CHAPTER 23

They were walking through tall grass when the rain started, a solid wall of water pouring on them like there was no tomorrow.

Rosita cursed. "Just what I needed!"

They walked for a quarter of a mile and finally found a ledge on the face of the cliff that jutted over a small niche in the side of the mountain. They ran under it, dripping.

"House of the gods, huh?" she said.

She had left Steve behind in her hurry to reach cover, and now she watched him limp through the curtain of water that ran down the roof of their sanctuary. Steve sat on the rock floor. "Looks like it will last a while."

"How's your leg?"

"I'll manage."

She pushed back the wet bangs sticking to her forehead. "Is there an emergency blanket in that kit?"

Steve rummaged in the bag and came up with two silver packets.

"Okay then, take off your clothes."

"Pardon?"

Rosita chuckled, undoing her blouse. "I am not making an attempt at your virtue." She dropped the wet garment on the ground and started undoing her belt. "You don't want to catch pneumonia, do you?"

"It's not the first soaking of the day," Steve said but started taking his clothes off.

"Cold wind, icy-cold rain. What a wonderful place, eh?" Standing in her bra and panties, Rosita opened one of the emergency blankets and shook it to unwrap it. "It's enough for both of us," she said.

She sat by Steve's side and pushed close to him, Sandra's medical bag pinched between them. "Here, tuck this end in, so there's no drafts."

She opened the second blanket and wrapped it around their backs, as an insulation between them and the rock wall. Sitting cross-legged, Steve wrapped himself in the foil blanket, and then tentatively put his arm around her shoulders. She nodded and moved closer. They sat there, the edge of the blanket up to their noses, the second blanket folded over their heads like a hood.

"Let's hope these things work," she sighed.

"Oh, they do. Physics and physiology are on our side." He stopped. "Why are you laughing?"

"Because you really can't stop lecturing me, eh?"

"Sorry."

She kept laughing. "I'm sort of getting used to it, really. Is there anything edible in that bag?"

She disappeared for a moment and re-emerged holding a bottle of water and a packet of cookies. The cardboard box was soggy, but the cookies inside were in a plastic wrapper. "Hooray, we won't starve."

They sat there, the rain the only sound, eating the cookies. The prairie was a sepia-colored blur as the sun went down.

Rosita removed the bag and got closer, leaning her head on Steve's shoulder. "Hell of a first date, isn't it?"

He laughed, choking on a piece of cookie.

"Yeah," he said, "the food is okay, but this place has gone to seed since the last time I was here."

"Look!" There was something moving in the distance. "Where the hell did they come from?"

"Some kind of ceratopsids," Steve said.

"Oh, I love it when you say that to me."

"Very funny."

"Dangerous?"

The beasts were built like small trucks, with a brown-green humped back and a massive head with horns. There were at least two dozen of them slowly walking through the rain, tightly packed, exchanging soft tweets and honking sounds. The rain ran down their warty hides but did not seem to bother them.

Steve took a deep breath. "Yes, because they are big and they are many. But they should be herbivores. If we keep our distance, don't make noise, and mind our own business they should ignore us. I guess."

"You guess?"

"Remember? Nobody ever saw these creatures alive."

They watched them go by for about an hour, grazing under the pouring rain, vague splotches of color in the receding light.

"This is the last time you take me out to one of your sucky movies," Rosita said. She held up a cookie. "Last one. Want it?"

"Be my guest."

#

As the rain got more intense and the night fell, Sandra found a hollow tree trunk, leaning against its neighbor, its roots exposed and dried up. They crawled in looking for shelter.

"At least it's dry," Mike said. He put down his passenger. Maria had started bleeding again, a large red-brown stain spreading on Mike's shirt.

"How bad is it?" he asked.

Sandra just shook her head. She cleaned the wound again, and wrapped it up in fresh rags. "She needs rest and sleep," she finally said. "And running through the jungle on a guy's back is not good. Not good at all. The bullet went clean through, and she lost a lot of blood."

"Any idea about who those men are?"

The doctor rested her head against the curve of the trunk and closed her eyes. "No," she breathed. "Mercenaries, professional soldiers. Friends of Mister Barreto, I thought. But then—"

The pilot grunted and stared at the jungle outside. "Why did they shoot her?"

"Your guess is as good as mine. Why did she run away?"

"Ditto."

Maria tossed in her sleep, her beautiful face pale and covered in sweat. She mumbled some words, and her hand found the cross hanging around her neck, and grasped it, her knuckles white.

"She must be very religious," Mike said.

Sandra passed a piece of cloth over the other woman's forehead.

#

They resumed their walk the next morning.

The rain had stopped during the night, and the prairie was quiet and empty.

"Where did those things go?" Rosita asked.

She had tied the emergency blanket around her neck, wearing it like a tin foil cape. Steve had rolled his own as tightly as he was able and carried it with the emergency kit.

"Probably enjoying the sun, squatting in the tall grass," he said. He scanned the horizon, frowning.

"No long-necked brontosaurs like in the movie? Those were kind of neat."

He grunted. "Unlikely."

Rosita eyed him, then chuckled. "C'mon!" she said. "I told you I like it when you lecture me."

Steve made a face. "First, a long neck means tall trees or deep lakes of which we have none here on this part of the plateau. And second, everything we've seen suggests this place favors smaller species."

"Why?"

"More energy efficient, and there is clearly a primary resources control of some sort." He glanced at her. "Not enough to eat for the herbivores, not enough space to expand."

Rosita made an interested face. "I see."

"Usually species are arranged in a sort of pyramid. A lot of herbivores at the bottom, and then less and less predators, arranged by size. It's because..."

A shadow passed over them.

They both looked up.

"What the hell is that?!"

A huge dragon glided towards them, big leathery wings outstretched, a long triangular head sporting row upon row of sharp white teeth.

"The top of the pyramid," Steve said, pushing her down.

The monster swooped down at them. They rolled through the grass as its talons snapped, and it rose again, its wings flapping furiously.

"Run!"

Rosita started through the grass, moving as close as possible to the cliff side.

"No!"

Steve watched her go, the sparkling tin foil stretched behind her in the breeze. Above them, the pterosaur banked and stretched its wings, preparing for a second run. It tilted its head imperceptibly. Steve started running after Rosita, the gash in his leg burning with each step. "The blanket!" he tried to shout.

A part of his brain registered how the pterosaur moved its head to evaluate the distance, then how the tendons in its taut wings contracted, twisting the wings and adjusting its trajectory. But he kept running and shouting. He heard the wings beat above them and the screech of the creature. Part of him wondered if the thing used sound location as the rest of him felt the shadow glide over him. Then the monster was braking its run, wings flapping, assuming a raptor's hunting position, claws forward, wings outstretched.

Time slowed down. Steve could see the tiger stripes along the beast's sides as it braked, wings stretched. The pale belly, the bright red of the snout. The teeth, the yellow eyes deep in their sockets. It reared up, hind legs pushed forward, like an eagle about to catch a salmon. Rosita screamed, fell to the ground. It tried to snatch her off, but she was too close to the rock wall, and its braking maneuver caught it short. Talons snapped, ripping the emergency blanket, but the thing screeched its frustration and flapped away, again gaining altitude.

With a curse, Steve dropped the bag, unfolded his emergency blanket, and started limping and shouting through the grass, away from the rocks, away from Rosita, waving his arms in the air, the silver and gold foil blanket like a banner.

The beast circled above, a black silhouette against the white of the low clouds. Again it aimed at its target, its head swinging this way and that. Then with a screech the pterosaur plunged toward him.

It was all a matter of timing. With a long incoherent scream, Steve let go of the blanket. The wind caught the light foil and carried it away. Steve huddled on the ground and watched as the flying monster shifted its balance and banked to the right, following the wind and the blanket. Its talons closed on the sparkling surface, and it started beating its wings again, flying away with its prey.

He watched it go, breathing hard.

Another shadow passed over him.

"That was very stupid," Rosita said.

She stood over him, the shredded foil blanket in her hand.

He sat up with a grunt. "That was effective."

Swiftly she stamped a peck on his cheek. "Courageous, mad, and completely stupid."

The pterosaur was gone. She helped him up, and then slowly walked back to where he had dropped the bag.

"Let's move," she said, picking it up. "It will not take long to realize it's been duped."

He watched her go, then limped slowly after her.

CHAPTER 24

"I'd say this is as good a spot as any other."

Rosita looked up at the cliff and then back at Steve. "You sure you can make it?"

The rock rose for about thirty feet above them, steep but not perfectly vertical. It was cracked and rugged, offering a number of handholds and footholds. This was the place where the scissor-fault Steve had described hinged. Two hundred yards more to the north and they would be on the tree-fringed edge of the tepui.

She adjusted the strap of the bag and gave him a look. "I go first," she said.

He made a theatrical gesture. "After you, madam."

Rosita snorted, shook her head, and put her foot on a small ledge.

"The good thing is," she said, "I am so short, that if I can find handholds, you can too."

She climbed up about five feet. Then she stopped, stretching flat against the rock surface for balance. "I've got an idea," she said, turning slightly.

"Nice spot to have one."

"You wait there," she said. "I go up, cut some vines..."

"Don't be silly".

He started looking for a good starting point. The sun was halfway up the mid-morning sky, and shadows were deceptive.

Then he turned suddenly. There was something moving in the trees, in the direction of the plateau's margin. Leaves rustled and small branches snapped, but he couldn't pinpoint the exact direction from where the newcomer approached. Cursing under his breath, Steve chose a promising-looking foothold and hauled himself up. The cut in his leg gave him a painful stab, but he ignored it.

"I'll race you," he said.

Rosita was already almost halfway to the top, following a climbing path about two feet to his right.

"Up here it gets smoother," she said.

He looked up. Again something rustled through the foliage behind them. Rosita heard it too.

"What was that?" she asked.

"Reason to climb faster."

"What?"

A rock, as big as a fist, slammed in the cliff face about two spans to the left of Steve's head. "Hey!"

This was not what he had expected. He remembered the blue lizards that had been trying to get Sandra. Small, smart bastards, fully capable of climbing.

A second projectile bumped into his back, hard enough to hurt but not to cause any real damage. With a grunt he pulled himself up using the strength of his arms, trying to make it to a small sandstone shelf.

There were noises. Gargling sounds and chirps and whistles.

He reached the rock ledge. It felt like it could support his weight. More rocks hit the cliff, one catching his injured leg and sending a kaleidoscope of pain up his spine.

"What are they?" Rosita called. A big chunk of stone exploded close to her. She gasped and turned her head, dust and shards flying at her eyes.

"Sandra's blue friends, I think. Keep climbing."

Steve refused to look back. His curiosity hurt more than his leg or his hands, but he forced it back and climbed up another foot, another three.

Then a shaft hit the rock and fell down rattling. Steve did a double take. Not a chunk of rock. A short spear, with a rough stone head. An artifact. A sophisticated artifact.

Against his best judgment, he stopped and turned.

Rosita screamed, a big rock hitting the back of her head. She lost her balance, lost her grip, and fell.

Steve did not think. He stretched, grabbed the woman's ankle as she fell. Rosita's weight sent a shock through his arm. He started falling backward. He slid the fingers of his left hand in a crack in the limestone, holding on for dear life, his right fist closed around Rosita's leg. The woman hung upside down, her back against the rock face, her arms dangling, the first aid bag caught in her chin and armpit. His muscles screamed. She was too heavy.

And beneath them, in a half-circle, stood about a dozen lizards, emerald green, with thick feather ruffles around their necks and down their thin arms. They were looking up at them with big, bulging eyes. Their scaly faces were painted in bright colors, and some of them carried short primitive spears. They kept at a safe distance and moved nervously, balancing on their hind legs, their tails stretched behind them.

Rosita groaned and opened her eyes.

One of the creatures moved forward and stabbed at her with his spear. Rosita screamed, thrashing. The spear punctured her dangling bag. The creatures jumped back. Two of them threw stones again.

"Pull me up!" she shouted.

Steve gritted his teeth, hauling her up, feeling like there was a knife plunging between his shoulder blades. He felt Rosita's hand on his leg, and pulled her closer. She kicked him in the face once, and then slid between him and the rock. Holding his grip in the fracture, he leaned back, giving her maneuvering room. She crept between him and the face of the cliff. She then grabbed his shirt and started rotating in a slow cartwheel, until she finally stood in front of him on the thin rock shelf. He pulled closer again, squeezing her against the rock, just as the stones started raining on them again.

He could feel her heart thumping against his chest. They were both breathing heavily. "Now what?" she asked.

And the sandstone ledge collapsed.

#

Jack took a bite of the sandwich and munched appreciatively.

"But I must say I don't get it," he said, brushing a few crumbs off his beard.

Schneider looked at him. "You don't?"

Jack shrugged and put down the sandwich. With his hands tied with a plastic strip, it was hard to eat and drink at the same time. Lots of pauses. He lifted the water bottle.

"What I mean is," he said after he had taken a long pull, "why don't you kill us straight away?"

He nodded at Terri, who sat, her hands tied, in the open side hatch of the chopper. She stared at him with wide eyes, then glanced at Schneider.

"I mean, you are going to kill us anyway, right? No sense in dancing around it. Whoever set this carnival in motion is not the sort of guy that likes witnesses. I don't know what you are looking for, but it's not us, and we are dead. But then, why not do it right now? Why the wait? Why let us," he lifted the bottle, "consume your provisions?"

"You think you are very smart, don't you, Mister Tanner?"

Jack shrugged. "You know what? I actually know I am pretty smart. Did tests, passed exams. Certainly smarter than you and your bunch of clowns. Oh," he huffed, "don't you give me the psycho Nazi wannabe evil look. Am I pissing you off?"

Schneider smirked. "You like very much the sound of your own voice, don't you?"

Jack laughed. "I am pissing you off. Poor little fucker. And on the other hand, what can you do, kill me? Oh, yeah, sorry, you're gonna kill me anyway, so why should I refrain from telling you that I think your mother should have taken precautions the day she fucked a goat?"

Schneider shook his head.

He stepped closer to Terri, smiled at her, and without warning slapped her, repeatedly, hard, making her cry out loud.

"You bastard!"

Jack stood but one of the goons with the gun hit him in the back, sending him face down in the dirt.

"I see you are the one that is, as you put it, pissed off."

"Untie me, you son of a bitch, and I'll show you just how pissed off I am."

Jack pushed himself up on his hands and knees.

Schneider kicked him in the ribs, winding him.

"You are not so smart, Mister Tanner." He turned. "Dragan, let's put Mister Tanner on display."

A hulking guy with ash-blond hair and scarred hands picked Jack up forcibly and dragged him away. Jack tried to resist and the man hit him squarely in the face with a ham-sized fist.

"You see, Mister Tanner, your friends out there have something I need. And you are going to convince them to bring it to me."

Jack spat some blood.

"Kill me, you moron!" he croaked. "Kill me now, or I swear I'll come for you!"

Schneider shook his head again, sighing. "How melodramatic," he said, smiling at Terri. Bruises were blossoming on the girl's face.

CHAPTER 25

The rock slide scattered the lizard-men. They let out a series of high whistles and ran back to the thick of the trees as a thick cloud of dust engulfed the rock face. The loose material piled up at the foot of the cliff, a few stray chunks rolling off in the sudden stillness.

Halfway up, Steve was still holding his fingers in the rock fracture, the edge of the crack cutting his skin as he dangled in the air, Rosita holding on to him. Eyes closed, teeth gritted, he fumbled trying to find a foothold of some kind. His boot caught a small crack, and he pushed himself up, relieving the weight from his arm with a grunt.

Rosita held onto him, one leg wrapped around his waist. She moved, found a foothold. She propped herself up and released him.

"Now you can let go," she said.

"What?"

She grinned and gave him a peck on the cheek. "You can let go of my ass, honey."

Steve's laugh turned into a fit of coughing. He found a different handhold. Rosita turned slowly, facing the cliff again, and she easily found points to use to move up. She put a foot on his shoulder, and one on his head, but soon she was climbing again.

He found a handhold and grasped it with his right. He pulled the left from the crack. It was like his hand had been released from a vice: the fingers were raw and bleeding, the nails broken, the palm crossed by a deep cut.

The rustling and the whistling in the bushes started again.

Steve closed his eyes for a moment, and then started up the rock face.

Rosita vaulted over the edge of the cliff and turned back to him. "Move it!"

#

Steve looked over the edge. The small band of lizard-men had grown, and now included a guy with a coelosurid skull as a cap, shaking a feathered staff.

Behind him, Rosita pulled the short spear out of her bag. The stone head was glassy, black, and roughly chipped. A piece of vegetal fiber held it in place.

"So instead of turning into birds, they turned into what? Kobolds?"

Steve turned to give her a look. "I would have never marked you for a D&D player."

"Hey, I was in high school, right? There's lots of stuff I can do that you wouldn't imagine."

"That sounds racy."

"Oh, shut up!"

He stood, moving his arms and trying to stretch his back.

"This is absolutely incredible," he mumbled. "There were some theories, of what would have happened, had the KT event never hit—"

Rosita was looking down on their attackers. She waved a hand. They threw stones at her. "Are we sure they can't climb up here?"

"Unlikely. Their arms and legs are not..."

A shaft quivered, stuck in a tree about three feet from where he stood.

"But they have bows and arrows, apparently."

"Okay, Mister Know-it-all, I think we better be going."

#

"She's not going to make it."

Mike stared at Sandra. "Are—"

Then he snapped his mouth shut. Of course she was sure. She was a doctor, after all.

In the first hours of the morning, Sandra Barillier's features were drawn, dark shadows under her eyes. She had collected her hair in a sort of bun held together by a pen, and the skin of her face was like wax. She was frustrated, he could see that. Not scared, but frustrated.

"I don't have what I need to stabilize her," she said, anger giving a new edge to her voice. "She lost a lot of blood, suffered massive trauma, she's going into shock and there's very little I can do out here. It's a miracle she survived the night."

He knew. He had seen what a high-speed 7.63 bullet could do to an unprotected human.

"What do you plan to do?"

Sandra sat back on her heels. "We need help."

"From those that shot her?"

Sandra cursed. "There's no other way. I need to do all I can to save her. And if this means," she gestured, "trying my luck with those men, I have to do it."

Mike could say nothing to that.

He stared at the young woman where she laid on a layer of

branches.

"Fine, let's go then."

"There's no need for you to come," she said. "You should go and try and join the Tanners, Rosy, and Terri. Wait and see what the newcomers will do."

Mike was about to speak when a long screeching sound, distinctly artificial, cut through the still air.

#

They drove four pickets in the ground and tied Jack to them, leaving him spread-eagled in the dirt, looking up at the sky.

A shadow fell over him.

"What's this, an Apache torture? Hondo?" Jack said. "You have watched too many bad movies—"

Schneider gave him a look of pity. "I am surprised you still have so much breath inside you."

Hernan Barreto walked up and stood behind Schneider, in a fresh shirt and with his arm in a professional cast.

"I see you're having it good, mister," Jack said.

Barreto ignored him. Schneider snapped his fingers, and one of the men handed him a microphone. A long stretch of cable connected it to a megaphone.

There was a loud, high-pitched, very unpleasant sound that cut through the silence. Then Schneider put his mouth close to the mic.

"Can you do 'Don't Stop Believing'?" Jack asked.

He got another kick in the ribs.

"I am a man of few words." Schneider's voice boomed.

Clouds of flying lizards flapped in panic, twittering furiously over the top of the trees.

"I want Maria Barreto. Bring her to me, and Mister Tanner will not suffer a long, painful death."

Again there was the loud feedback screech of the amplifiers.

Schneider looked up to the sky.

"Then I will do the same to the girl," he said.

One of his men turned off the amp with a loud thumping sound. Everything was silent for a long minute.

In the distance, a loud growl rose, echoing like thunder, and was soon joined by a chorus of similar calls.

The man backing Schneider looked at each other.

"Fuck, man," Jack said, laughing despite the pain. "Looks like you attracted the attention of the wrong crowd."

Schneider marched away.

The growl and howls rose in volume.

#

"I am moved," Hernan said, hastening to stay by his side, "but are you sure this is really necessary to save my wife?"

Schneider stopped and gave him one long look. "Dragan," he said, without turning.

"Yes, boss?"

"Take this moron out of my sight."

Barreto gasped.

"And gag him."

Barreto tried to protest, but the big mercenary's grip made his voice die in his throat. Schneider watched as the man was marched toward the carcass of the Pilatus, looking over his shoulder with pleading eyes and a pale face.

"Boss!"

"What now?"

One of the men pointed back at the choppers. "Sergio's back, Boss. I mean, Ortega. He is in bad shape."

Schneider followed him back.

More animal growls rose from the jungle, closer, louder.

Behind him, Jack Tanner laughed. "They are coming, you bastard!" the prisoner shouted. "Just pray they get you before I do!"

#

Rosita cursed.

There were two bodies, lying in the middle of the clearing. Two badly mangled carcasses in fatigues laying in the trampled grass.

"None of ours," she said.

Steve limped to the closest body. "Stay away," he said. "This one's been partially eaten."

Rosita snorted. "Like I was some delicate flower!"

She stopped by Steve's side and crouched down. "Here—" She lifted the limp body of a blue lizard, holding it by the tail between thumb and forefinger. "Sandra's friends strike back."

Steve was scanning the margin of the clearing. "I think we better get going," he said. "And save the debate on the connection between intelligence and aggression for later."

Rosita smiled without humor. The man was learning.

She dropped the dead lizard and rubbed her hands on her trousers.

"Gimme a minute." She pulled the AK-74 from under the dead body. She checked it and armed it.

She gave Steve a look. "Well? I told you there's a lot you don't know about me."

"I'm impressed."

"Well, stop being impressed and see if the other guy's got any spare magazines."

Steve trudged to the other body and with a grimace checked his belt and the pockets of his ripped vest.

"They did not just kill and eat them," he said, walking back to her. "They also looted the bodies."

She arched her eyebrows and he showed her a torn pack of cigarettes. The teeth marks were evident.

"Cigarette smoking cannibal blue lizards," she said, standing up. She took the two magazines he had found, and slipped them in the utility belt she had taken off the body.

"Does the radio still work?"

She picked it up. She thumbed through the selection until she caught a voice.

"Talk to me, Tango 1--"

"Looks like it does."

Steve clipped it to his belt. "This way we'll hear what our strange rescuers are saying."

There was a long, whining sound in the distance, and then a sound like a voice booming, impossible to understand.

"What—?"

"Somebody's using an amplifier."

The booming voice spoke for a few moments, and then it fell silent with another screech. After two heartbeats, a beast roared in the forest, followed by another, and then another. Soon, a thundering chorus of predator calls echoed through the trees.

They felt, more than saw or heard, the big animals start moving in the direction of the plane.

"I have a bad feeling about this," Steve said.

CHAPTER 26

Ortega sat by Bravo 1. His fatigues were torn. He bled from a number of small cuts. He had lost his weapon. He looked tired and scared. This gave Schneider pause. Ortega was not the sort of man who scared easily. Or who dropped his gun.

"What happened?"

"We were attacked," Ortega replied. His voice was raspy, his lips cracked from lack of drink.

"By who?"

The man shook his head, passing a hand across his lined features, like he had a hard time believing it himself. "Small lizards, about this tall. Blue. They caught us with our pants down."

"Mick and Tim?"

Ortega glanced at him. "Gone."

Schneider frowned. Two men gone, two men missing. "We weren't informed of the odds," he said. "Aggressive fauna was not part of the deal—"

Ortega was not listening. "One of those little fuckers shot at us. He picked up a gun and shot at us."

Schneider looked at the guy standing there. Marin, he remembered, or something like that. The guy just shrugged.

He patted Ortega on a shoulder. "Get some rest."

The old soldier dropped his water bottle and shrugged off his hand. "I'm not going crazy, boss." He stood. "Those animals are smart. Maybe not the big one we shot down here, but the small ones are smart, and evil. This place is dangerous."

Schneider nodded. "Sure."

Ortega snorted. "Do you remember that night in Antananarivo, in 2010?" he asked, coming closer. "The bar, and that guy with his pet monkey? Weird critter with big eyes?"

Schneider nodded again.

He knew what Ortega was getting at. The night in the Malagasy bar, drinking, smoking and playing cards. And the man with the pet monkey. The strange animal with the round head and the big bulging eyes, and the fur like velvet. The thing that liked to lick the rum shots clean, and everybody laughed. Until it picked up a 1911A from the table and fired a shot.

"Nobody ever said the thing was a trained sharpshooter," Ortega was saying, "but it shot Felix T dead, and would have shot somebody else had I not knifed it. And I'm not saying I met a platoon of lizard riflemen. Only that those fucking animals are just as smart as a Madagascar chipmunk. And just as dangerous. And there's a lot of them."

"Get some rest. By tomorrow morning everything will be over."

#

Jack realized something was happening when he heard and then saw the men in the camp get moving. Then Sandra stopped by his side. She was carrying Maria Barreto in her arms. The girl was unconscious, or dead. One arm dangling limp, her head cradled against Sandra's shoulder. Blood stained Sandra's tan shirt, and Maria's red dress was turning a dark brown in places.

"What the hell are you doing?" he croaked. Or something similar. His voice came out like a raspy gurgle, and he worked his jaw, trying to get some spit in his dry mouth.

"Are you all right?" she asked.

"Go away," he tried. "They will kill us."

But Sandra's jaw was set, and she was staring with derision at the approaching silhouette of Schneider.

The leader of the mercenaries stopped in front of Sandra.

"Doctor." He smirked.

"She is very weak," Sandra said. "I need a clean place, and access to your medical supplies—"

"We will take care of Mrs. Barreto."

He took a step forward, placed a finger under the woman's chin and lifted her head. His eyes flared.

"Where is her cross?"

Sandra stared at him like he was completely crazy. "What?"

"The chain, on her neck."

Sandra glanced at Jack where he was stretched on the ground. "I have no idea—"

Schneider's smirk became a snarl. "This woman was wearing a chain around her neck."

"And then your men shot her. And she stumbled through the jungle, and crawled, and almost bled to death. She is bleeding to death right now—"

Schneider gestured and one of his men came and picked the limp body of Maria Barreto from Sandra's arms.

"We'll see to her injuries," Schneider said. "You come this way."

#

"The chick's in bad shape," Shaw said. He was the team's surgeon, and he was used to seeing people with gun wounds. "I don't think she'll make it."

"Can she talk?"

Shaw gave his commander a look.

Schneider grunted. "Do you think the woman can help you? The doctor, I mean."

Sandra sat by one of the choppers, hands bound with a plastic strip. She was talking with Terri.

The surgeon glanced at her. "I have my doubts we can do anything—"

"I need to talk to the bitch—"

"Not likely."

He turned to one of the men. "Bring the doctor here."

He stared at Shaw. "You wake the girl and you get me to talk to her for two minutes," he said in a low voice. "Then you can let her die for all I care."

The guard pushed her and Sandra stumbled.

"Doctor Barillier." Schneider smirked. "You and my man will patch up Mrs. Barreto."

Sandra eyed Shaw, who shrugged.

"What about Jack Tanner?"

"What about him?"

"You've got what you wanted—"

"Not yet. It is essential I speak with Mrs. Barreto—"

"For her to tell you where she dropped her cross."

Schneider just stared at her.

"Do I get to use my hands?" she asked.

Shaw cut her restraints. "The bullet got in and made a mess," he started explaining, leading her to the other chopper and the stretcher on which Maria lay. "It hit a bone and started spinning. There's a hole as big as a fist in her side. I stitched her up, gave her plasma—p"

Schneider watched them go and nodded to his man to follow them.

#

"Holy shit!"

Animals slowly ambled through the tall grass, heads moving left to right and back again as they grazed the long green leaves. Horns pointing at the sky, large bone shields like lace collars in some old painting.

"Fall back," Schneider said, in a low voice. "Form a perimeter around the choppers."

Ortega nodded, but it took him a moment to shake out of his fascination for the herd. He started shouting commands.

"Move it, you lazy bastards!"

One of the creatures looked up, curious about the sound.

It honked once, like a big pig.

"Be ready, but hold your fire," Ortega was shouting. "As long as they stay away from us and the helicopters, we are fine. Don't want to start a stampede or something."

"What about that guy?" Marin asked. He nodded at the place where Jack Tanner was tied.

Ortega turned and stared at Schneider.

Schneider just shook his head.

"We leave him there," Ortega said. "He'll take his chances with the monsters."

"They seem to be herbivores," Marin said. "Like cows. I doubt they'll attack him."

"But they can trample him."

The men were regrouping, trading glances and talking.

"We are not paid to chat," Ortega barked. "Close ranks and keep your wits about you."

He moved along the line. "Like Marin here said, they're just big cows. And we ain't scared of cows, right?"

Someone laughed.

More dinosaurs were now looking their way, attracted by the sound of voices. They kept pulling bunches of grass with their beaks and slowly munching on them. But they were attentive, their small eyes roaming the field to come back to where the humans and their machines were sitting.

The dinosaurs honked and chirped at each other and slowly advanced through the grassland.

CHAPTER 27

The T. Rex roared its frustration and thrashed the undergrowth with its tail.

"Nasty brute," Rosita said.

They were standing at the lip of one of the fractures that cut through the plateau, filled with thick mist and the calls of unseen creatures. The big predator was on the other side.

It growled again.

"He can smell us," Steve said.

"How do you know he's not a she?"

"Good point. But *my* point is, according to some models they were shortsighted."

He bent and picked up a chunk of rock.

"What are you doing?"

Steve pulled his arm back and threw the stone as far as he could. It crashed through the foliage. The Rex did not stir.

"Testing its hearing."

Rosita's eyes goggled, and she was about to say something when Mike O'Reilly emerged from the underbrush, breathing heavily, his clothes soaking wet. He was pale, panting, his eyes wide. Rosita thought he looked close to a heart attack. He stood about one hundred yards from the dino, which turned sharply towards him.

"There you are!" Mike shouted.

The Rex growled and bent down, peeping through the branches and the mist.

Rosita hissed and unslung the AK-74.

"Run!" she shouted.

Mike looked at them.

The Rex charged with a bellow.

#

Mike saw the big lizard crash through the undergrowth and raised his gun instinctively, plugging it with six bullets, before he threw himself to one side. The beast ignored the shots and nimbly turned to the side, its jaws snapping one foot away from Mike's head.

Mike rolled on the ground, the useless revolver still in his hand, and the rattle of an automatic weapon cut through the air.

The dinosaur stood in all its height, roaring, and turned, his side a ruin of ripped hide and mangled muscle.

Mike scrambled over the soft floor of the jungle, and threw himself behind the trunk of a big conifer. The dino ran its claws on the bark of the tree as it moved around it.

Mike stood. On the other side of the chasm, Rosita was struggling to fit a new magazine in her assault rifle.

The dinosaur lunged. Mike cursed, threw the gun at it, and jumped away, vaulting over a fallen tree trunk. He landed with a grunt, his heart drumming in his throat. The dino slammed into the fallen tree. Mike took an instinctive step back. The ground crumbled under his foot. He did a half turn and plunged into the abyss.

The monster threw its head back and let out a sound halfway between a howl and a screech, and a hail of bullets slammed into its chest and neck. The creature tottered, screeched once again, and crashed to the ground, its legs contracting, its tail swinging one last time.

#

Steve and Rosita stood, stricken, at the edge of the crack, staring at the place where Mike had been.

She cupped her hands around her mouth and shouted his name, at the top of her lungs. There was no response but the echo of her voice between the walls of the canyon and a chorus of chirps and tweets from down below.

"Shit," she breathed.

Steve watched her crouch down, her face in her hands.

"Of all the stupid old fools," she gulped.

Steve bent his knees with a grimace and placed a hand on her shoulder.

"We must go," he said. "We must find the others."

She nodded and rubbed her hands on her cheeks.

Then Mike O'Reilly's voice sounded through the mist, crying for help.

"The bastard!" she exclaimed. She jumped to her feet and started running, Steve limping behind her.

#

Mike O'Reilly was hanging for dear life to a thick vine flush against the rock face. Looking up, he could see the lip of the cut, maybe six feet above him. Six feet or six thousand, his early attempt at climbing had resulted in a fall of dirt and pebbles, and him sliding down one foot more.

He shouted for help again, then concentrated on his breathing.

The trick, he told himself, was to keep breathing, slowly and regularly. Keep the heart under control, ignore the piercing pain in his chest. Ignore the pain in his hands, in his shoulders.

He took another long breath.

The air was wet and smelled of humidity and decay.

Breathe slowly.

Slow down your pounding heart.

A small bird, like a sparrow, its feathers bright orange, landed on a rock spur by his face, and stared at him, bending its neck with open curiosity.

Mike smiled despite himself.

He moved his feet, trying to find some support, to ease the pain in his back.

The bird chirped, then flew away.

His hands were on fire.

With the tip of his left foot, he found some hold and tried to lean into it. A chunk of rock detached from the rock face and fell forever. There was a splash.

Mike grabbed the vine tighter.

Then, a belt buckle jangling against the rock, a makeshift rope crawled down to him.

He looked up and saw Rosita staring down at him.

"We're here, old man!" she shouted.

Old man.

Mike grunted and grasped the belt.

#

Steve had dug footholds in the dirt to help him support the weight of the pilot. When Mike grabbed their line, he was braced and ready, and still he felt like his arms were being pulled from their sockets.

Rosita started pulling the rope, slowly.

They had tied together their belts and the emergency bag strap. The rope was long enough, but Steve was afraid it would snap at the junctions.

"Okay, he's coming," Rosita said.

Steve nodded, gritted his teeth, and helped her drag the old man up.

Finally, O'Reilly's head appeared above the edge. He was red in the face, soaked in sweat. He let go of the makeshift rope with his right hand and clawed at the dirt, trying to pull himself up. Rosita let go of the rope and grabbed his wrist, his arm.

They finally hauled him up, and he lay face down for a long minute, his face in the dirt, breathing in gasps, his legs still dangling in the void.

Then they helped him up, and Steve handed him a canteen. "Drink slowly," he said.

The pilot nodded and poured the contents of the metal bottle down his throat like there was no tomorrow.

CHAPTER 28

The man in combat fatigues placed his hand on Sandra's shoulder, almost tenderly. "There was not much you could do," he said.

She shrugged him off, and then felt guilty for doing so. Human kindness was such a rare commodity; one should not despise it like this.

"She was so young," she whispered.

Maria Barreto lay stretched out on the chopper's cabin floor that had doubled as an impromptu infirmary. Now empty of life, the beautiful body of Maria looked to Sandra like it was no longer so beautiful or so young. There was a wax-like hollowness to the once beautiful face, and her body was relaxed, slack, a dead thing.

The man in fatigues nodded and took a deep breath.

"I'll handle him, don't worry," he said in a low voice.

Sandra frowned.

The man turned and walked to where the leader of the band was standing. They started talking. She could see the boss did not like the news.

She pulled the thin emergency blanket over Maria's face, wrapping her in a tin foil shroud.

The boss, Schneider, pushed the surgeon back and paced toward her.

"I am very disappointed," he said. His voice was harsh, his face drawn. He was clearly a man that did not like being disappointed.

"I guess Maria is, too," she replied.

He snorted. "Did she talk? Before she died?"

Sandra shook her head. "No, she never revived. Too massive a trauma—"

He stared her in the face. His eyes were dead. They had the same cold intelligence of the small blue lizards. Not a man. Just a predator.

"And you have no idea where her chain and cross may be?"

She turned towards the forest. "Somewhere in there," she said. "Can you get your men to help bury her?"

He kept staring at her. "You never noticed her trinket?"

Sandra smirked. "Maria Barreto was not a woman to wear trinkets. Her bubble bath cost as much as champagne."

"You knew her well?"

"We spent a few hours together, in the last few days."

She slipped her hand in her pocket.

"What's in your pocket?"

She arched her eyebrows. Then she pulled out her pack of cigarettes.

He barked an order and had one of his men take Sandra to where Terri was sitting. They tied her hands again, and she sat on the ground, sharing her cigarette with the American girl.

Maria Barreto's silver cross burned in her pocket like a red hot coal.

#

"Ceratopsids."

Rosita sighed theatrically. "You keep saying that to me, I'll get ideas."

Mike eyed first Steve and then Rosita, and then snorted. "This is not a high school field trip, kids," he grunted.

"But those *are* ceratopsids. A full herd of them."

"Nasty bastards," Mike grumbled. "It was one of those that dislodged the plane and pushed it there. That idiot Barreto spooked them and they stampeded."

Steve was looking at the place where his brother was still tied to the ground. Five hundred yards away, the mercenaries were grouped close by the choppers. Mike couldn't see Barreto or Sandra, nor the Nazi that led that band of cutthroats.

"The way I see it," Rosita said, "if those guys have any say in the matter, we are not going to leave this place."

"Not alive, at least," Mike agreed.

"Any idea of what they are after?"

Mike shrugged. "The Barretos, I'd say."

He turned and gave Steve a look. Steve scanned the herd as it advanced slowly through the grass.

"They are herbivores," Steve said, almost talking to himself. "I guess they scare easily."

"I was much more scared than them," Mike replied. "Nasty brutes."

Steve scratched his beard. "I think I've got an idea."

#

The sun beat down on Jack Tanner.

His eyes closed, he still saw the red of the glaring sun through his eyelids. He could feel the skin of his face get tight as the sun baked it, and his mouth was like sandpaper. He sucked on his tongue, trying to salivate enough to wet his gums, his lips. They had used nylon strips to tie him to the pickets, and the plastic cut into his wrists.

He wondered what had been of his brother. He hoped he was safe somewhere with the little Japanese girl, but he knew it was unlikely. These men were professionals. He had heard gunshots in the distance. And then there were the beasts.

And Schneider.

Cold, ruthless bastard that slapped girls around.

He breathed in the warm air, eyes closed, and forced himself to hold on. Because he would get out of this bind.

And then he would get Schneider.

#

For the hundredth time, Mike measured the distance separating the edge of the forest and the wreck of the Pilatus. The sun was still high in the sky, and the ceratopsids were packing as much grass as they could, mowing the green and yellow leaves with mechanical precision. One of them held its head up while the others grazed for stretches of ten to fifteen minutes. Then one of its companions would stop, look up, and the lookout would resume its meal.

The men by the choppers walked up and down, weapons ready, tiny shapes at the far end of the esplanade.

With a heavy breath and a curse, Mike started running.

He kept low, moving swiftly through the brushes and then out in the open, sprinting as best as he could to the remains of his plane.

The idea, nagging at the back of his brain, that Steve Tanner's plan was the stupidest suicidal idea he had ever heard faded as he focused on speed and carefulness. Legs pumping, heart beating, he covered the distance without looking toward the men or the dinosaurs.

What was that old kid game? If you don't see them they won't see you.

Then he was in the shadows behind the wrecked body of the Pilatus. He stood, his back against the contorted metal, catching his breath. He passed a hand over his forehead and then sneaked in through the back.

#

From where she crouched in the bushes, Rosita could see Terri and Sandra where they sat on the ground by the helicopter.

Two men guarded them, one standing by the girls and smoking while the other paced up and down between the forest and the choppers. He held onto his gun like a shipwrecked sailor to a life jacket, and kept casting nervous glances at the trees and the shadows.

Rosita could understand him. The undergrowth was alive with calls and movement, rustling and cracking with the passage of animals. It was like all of the crazy fauna of this place was coming over to get a look at the final show.

And maybe take part in it.

From behind the tree where she was squatting, she could not see the Pilatus. The dinos were hazy, humpback shapes in the distance. She could barely see where Jack was strapped to the ground.

She could also see the foil-wrapped body of Maria Barreto that had been laid on the ground, about ten yards behind the choppers. Two men dug a grave.

She waited, cradling her AK-74, and wondering how all of this would play out.

Then she saw Steve walk over to the place where his brother was. And all hell broke loose.

#

"What the heck—?"

It came out as a croak, Jack's chapped lips stretched over his teeth.

His brother knelt down by his side and quickly cut the plastic strip holding his left hand.

The mercenaries were shouting.

"Go away, you fool!"

Steve handed him a water bottle and grinned, moving to free his right hand. "Easy," he said.

There was a shot in the distance. A bullet zinged past.

The camp came alive. His right hand free, Jack sat up and sucked on the water, looking that way.

"Move it," he said, "they won't miss the next time."

"Easy," Steve repeated. "I brought the cavalry."

And a ball of fire exploded in the tall grass.

The dinosaurs looked up as one, bellowing their calls in panic. And started running.

"Come," Steve said.

He helped his brother up, and they ran to the cover of the trees.

The men with the guns were too busy to shoot them.

#

There were still seven parachute rockets in the emergency supplies bag. Mike fired four in quick sequence, keeping the tubes low so that the projectiles would hit the ground in the tall grass at the back of the dinosaurs.

When the first one went off, the beasts were startled, but did not react. Too stupid or slow or whatever.

But the second did the trick. The wet grass did not burst into flames, but the rockets spread a red glow that was reflected in the thick clouds of black smoke rising from the impact sites. The smell of slow burning grass and chemicals and the red light did the trick. By the time the third rocket landed, the dinos were moving, honking and bellowing, their massive legs pounding the ground, and they ran like a wave towards the helicopters. They coursed through the wet grass, a thin mist of droplets dispersing and wreathing them in a rainbow aura.

It was beautiful and scary.

Mike fired the fourth rocket, trying to corral the beasts and direct their stampede. Then the men with the guns started firing, and at that point the dinos did not require any more push. They screamed in fury and charged.

Mike pushed the three remaining rocket tubes in his belt and started running back to the forest. He hoped the Tanners had gotten out of the way fast.

CHAPTER 29

Rosita had rehearsed her actions ten thousand times, so when chaos broke loose, and the men started firing at the dinos, and the beasts were careering towards the parked helicopters, she knew what she was doing, and was so extraordinarily dispassionate about it, she almost frightened herself. Like playing Doom.

She stood and shot the man in front of her.

He was staring at the incoming dinos, scared witless, and never saw the bullet coming. She hit him under his right arm. His finger contracted on the trigger as he fell and he fired a short burst aimlessly.

Rosita ran through the underbrush and toward the helicopter. She shot the man guarding Sandra and Terri, a three-round burst at the belly. He doubled over and fell back, and the girls gasped and screeched.

"Come on!" she shouted, pulling the strap of the assault rifle over her head.

The two prisoners staggered to their feet and jumped on the chopper just as Rosita sat on the pilot's seat and took a deep breath, trying to find her bearings in the crowd of dials, buttons, lights.

She handed the AK-74 to Sandra. "Can you use it?"

"Not with my hands tied."

A bullet ricocheted on the body of the chopper.

"Here!"

Rosita started the main engine as she rummaged in her pocket. She handed Terri a Swiss Army knife.

People started screaming.

Rosita put the headphones on and turned around.

There was a Rex, standing over the man she had shot. It lifted its head, its maws dripping red, and they stared at each other for a single heartbeat.

Behind her, Sandra was shooting.

"Hold on tight, we're leaving!"

#

"We should have brought hand grenades," Ortega said, snapping another magazine in his rifle. He turned and realized he was alone.

He cursed and fired into the incoming mass in the vain hope they'd disperse, or open and pass him by.

But just like his men, the animals were scared—too scared.

Then a ceratopsid was upon him. It swung its head, like it wanted to push this new obstacle aside. The beast bled from a dozen punctures and still ran full tilt. Its head smashed into Ortega's side. Ribs snapped, and the man howled as he was pushed on the ground. A second dino trampled him, barely noticing.

#

Schneider felt the hum of the rotor and turned in time to see Bravo 2 take off, the two prisoners in the back cabin, the clamshell doors in the back still hanging open, boxes of equipment falling out.

The chopper flew in an uncertain, wobbly way, aiming at the jungle.

Schneider cursed and started towards Bravo 1, in time to see the big squat chopper totter on its landing gear, and then tilt to fall on its side, the dinosaurs pushing against it. Men who had been trying to get on board now ran back, screaming. The big rotor snapped, and one of the men cried as the machine rolled over him, squashing him.

There was a roar, close.

A big lizard stared at him, maws bloodied, tail sweeping. Not one of the squat herbivores. One like the first they had seen. Schneider picked up a rifle from the ground and started shooting, full auto, the stock against his hip. The bullets slammed in the chest of the creature, and it staggered back. Then it charged.

Schneider fired again.

#

There were alarms screaming and lights flashing everywhere. The story of her life. Rosita found the central switch and shut the klaxons off.

The Hip was swinging this way and that, heavy on the commands. "We've got the back bay open!" Sandra shouted, a hand on her shoulder.

Rosita snorted. Passengers, always complaining about the service. "This is a Russian chopper," she shouted back. "No servos. The things are open, and stay open."

She did an ample curve over the grassland, trying to get her bearings.

The clearing was a few hundred yards away.

She pointed in that direction, concentrating on keeping the Hip as steady as possible.

#

"So what's the plan?" Jack asked.

They were running through the undergrowth, pushing branches and brushes out of their way.

"Rosita will pick us up," Steve panted.

"Rosita—?"

Steve stopped, leaning against a tree, and nodded, out of breath. "She is stealing one of their choppers."

Jack stared at him and then started laughing. "And the fucking dinos—"

"A diversion."

They both turned as Mike O'Reilly broke through the shrubbery, his shirt soaked in sweat. "You guys all right?"

Jack nodded.

"Nice fireworks," Steve said.

A Rex roared and crashed through the vegetation, jaws snapping, pointing toward them.

Steve pushed Jack away and rolled behind the tree.

The big lizard slammed against the trunk, roaring, its tail cutting through the brushes, throwing fern branches all over the place. It twittered in frustration and turned to Jack, who was on one knee, trying to stand and get out of the way.

The monster lunged, jaws open. A blast of fetid breath choked Jack, and he stared at the mouth about to close on him. He pushed away, knowing it was too close, too fast.

A red fireball exploded in the dinosaur's maw, and the monster snapped its mouth instinctively, and reared, bellowing in pain and fury. Shaking its head, it tried to spit the fire burning in his throat. All control lost, it pranced about, slamming into the trees and screaming.

Mike took Jack by an arm and they ran, Steve joining them.

The clearing loomed in front of them, and they had no time for playing.

#

Three bat-winged shadows crossed the path of the Hip, flying in formation, stark against the pale sky and the clouds.

Rosita cursed.

"We've got company," she shouted, trying to see where the pterodactyls had flown. The clearing was in front of them, about two hundred yards away, coming fast.

Too low, too fast.

Rosita checked the instruments as one of the monsters appeared to her right, matching speed with the chopper. It opened its long snout and screeched, but the sound was lost in the thunder of the engine. Behind Rosita, Sandra wrapped a seatbelt around her left arm, and then balanced close to the side door to take aim with the rifle. By her side, Terri held on, pale, squinting against the wind. She still held Rosita's Swiss Army knife.

Sandra fired a short burst, and the flying monster banked, braking with its wings, putting some distance between itself and the gun.

"Hold tight, we're landing!" Rosita shouted.

Sandra was about to reply when Terri screamed.

The Hip jumped and the engine groaned. Sandra turned and caught a flash of a long neck, a long triangular beak lined with teeth that closed on Terri's upper body, an elongated head that snapped back as the pterodactyl pushed back from the door behind her and flew away.

Sandra pulled the trigger, and the gun clicked. Empty.

#

The men emerged in the clearing of the blue lizards just as the chopper flew over them, rolling wildly, the pterodactyl hanging on the chopper's side, its head and shoulders rammed through the hatch, its leathery wings folded, its body pushed inside the helicopter.

Mike stopped and gasped. "Jesus Christ!"

Then the beast wriggled out, its wings extending and beating frantically, and it flew away, careful to avoid the rotating blades of the flying machine. There was a body in its mouth, thrashing and screaming.

The Hip overshot the clearing, swinging this way and that, and was gone. The three men stood, dumbstruck, watching the sky.

"Now what?" Jack asked.

"She'll get back," Steve said.

"No, I meant about those."

Jack pointed at the small troop of blue lizards that marched, tightly packed, toward them.

CHAPTER 30

Schneider stopped, listening.

He could hear the sound of the chopper somewhere in front of him. Behind him the shouts and shots had ceased, and the pounding sound of the dinosaur stampede was waning.

That was a case closed, but he was not going to let himself go. He had a mission, and a helicopter to catch.

He pulled his pistol out and ran toward the sound of the rotors.

#

"What the hell happened?"

Sandra slipped in the second pilot's seat and shook her head. "Terri—"

"Shit!"

Rosita put the Hip in a tight bank, going back to the clearing. She thought she had caught a glimpse of Steve and the others as they flew over.

She stopped over the clearing, concentrating on putting the bird down gently.

Beneath them, animal calls and human screams were lost in the noise of the engine.

#

The parachute rocket exploded in the middle of the lizards, causing them to disperse with furious chattering. Steve and Jack had armed themselves with thick branches and waited at Mike's sides.

They did not have long to wait. With a chorus of whistles and screeches, the small lizards were on them from all sides, using talons and bites, while others remained behind and pelted the men with stones. Jack turned his makeshift weapon this way and that, trying to keep them at bay the best he could. Steve cursed and pulled one of the animals away from over his shoulder, throwing it back at its friends. Mike kicked a blue lizard as it came close, and then lunged to the side, trying to avoid another hell-bent on biting his calf. He dodged Jack's next swing, shouting a warning.

Jack stopped and turned, and one of the creatures was on his back, shredding his shirt with its talons, tracing lines of fire on his back. Mike grabbed the thing and pulled it away, all the while kicking away his other attacker. One of the little monsters jumped at his crotch, and he intercepted it with his knee. The creature grabbed his leg and tried to bite into his thigh.

With a roar, Steve caught one of the creatures as it jumped at his face. The lizard bit hard in his hand, and Steve grabbed its neck and snapped it. Two other beasts faced him and stopped, chirping in horror. Intelligent as monkeys, he thought. They jumped at him. And vengeful. He used the dead lizard to beat his attackers, holding them back, the scaly body like a bludgeon.

Then a sound of thunder and a howling wind were upon them, and the little creatures were gone, leaving behind their dead.

The Hip landed with a groan, and Rosita shouted at them to run.

#

Jack jumped through the hatch and turned, extending one hand. Steve grabbed it and his brother hauled him up, and then both bent and stretched to grab Mike and pull him in.

In the cockpit, Rosita and Sandra were shouting. The men were bleeding and disheveled, but they were alive, and that was all that mattered. Mike put his foot on the lower margin of the hatch and grinned as the brothers helped him up.

Then a gunshot rang, like the striking of a gong, and Mike's eyes widened, as in surprise. A red stain blossomed in the back of his shirt, and the Tanners hauled him up, bleeding.

Schneider stood at the margin of the clearing, in perfect pistol shooting position, one arm folded behind his back, the other stretched in front of him.

Steve knelt down, checking the old man, and Sandra left her seat and joined him, pushing him back. Jack remained in the frame of the hatch, staring at Schneider.

"He's not breathing!" Sandra shouted over the noise of the rotors.

In the distance, the mercenary bent his elbow, and then stretched his arm again, a wild grin on his ruddy face. He took careful aim at Jack's head.

The two men stared each other in the eye across the clearing. Jack squared his shoulders, like he was inviting Schneider to shoot him.

Schneider's smile widened. He saw Jack move his lips.

Schneider smirked.

#

"Look behind you, you idiot," Jack said, softly.

Schneider could not hear him, of course.

Too distant, too concentrated, too intent on shooting him.

And what could he do anyway?

The tyrannosaurus snapped at him, biting into his chest and his shoulder, crushing the rib cage and the lungs, and then straightened and shook its head furiously, wrecking the body like it was a puppet.

Then the floor pushed up under Jack's feet, and the Hip was taking flight. The trees rushed by them, and then they were in the sky, surrounded by a cloud of small birds, or lizards, or whatever they were.

Jack did not care anymore.

He sat down on one of the passenger benches, spent.

#

"Steve, honey, can you do something for the back hatch?"

Steve glanced at Sandra, busy trying to revive Mike and then, with a nod to his brother, he staggered to the cargo bay, holding tight to the webbing along the walls.

The two convex doors were open, two simple struts holding them in position. Steve frowned. There were ropes dangling from each door that could be used to pull them closed. He looked down at the forest running under them, and just as he took the next step forward, the forest ended, and they were flying over a white fluffy stretch of clouds. He felt a moment of vertigo.

Wrapping the webbing around his left wrist, he stretched forward and tried to grab the rope on the left door. He came short on the first attempt, so he took a step forward and stretched some more.

There was a deafening screech and a sharp triangular head shot past him. Steve shouted and turned to face the wall, grabbing the webbing with both hands, as the pterodactyl pushed itself into the cargo hold of the Hip, its tall cranial crest brushing the ceiling, its wings folded, the small claws at the tips grabbing the floor and pulling it forward. It had smelled blood, a voice in Steve's mind reasoned, while the man was pushed against the metal, the rancid odor of wild animal suffocating him. It had feathers, he noticed, at the margin of its wings.

Jack pushed Sandra back and looked around in search of a weapon. Rosita looked back over her shoulder, cursed, and pulled the controls. The Hip started to climb at a steep angle as she tried to dislodge the monster. The engine revved up, fighting gravity and aerodynamics.

The creature screeched, and snapped at Jack, who had backed

against the wall. He used Sandra's rifle like a club, smashing the stock in the monster's head.

Steve tightened his grip and then started kicking the pterodactyl in the side, using both legs. The beast rattled and roared and screeched, moving its head this way and that.

Sandra tried to pull Mike back, away from the creature's jaws. She grasped him by the belt and pulled. Her hand ran over the last rocket tube.

Rosita banked and pulled up, and banked again. The monster slid back, its claws grating on the steel of the floor. The webbing detached from its supports under Steve's weight and he rolled back and slid out of the hatch, still grabbing the net of nylon strips that now dangled behind the chopper like a loose tail. He shouted, kicking in the void.

Sandra waited for the monster to scream its fury at her, and then pulled the cord. The tube heated in her hand and made a sound like a cork shooting out of a champagne bottle. The pterodactyl shut its maw and the rocket hit it in the right eye, exploding in a scarlet ball of light and heat.

The creature screeched, thrashing, and right then Rosita pulled up and banked again, and the body of the flying lizard slid out of the cargo bay, and fell, disappearing in the clouds, crumpled like a dead leaf.

The Hip leveled, and Steve cursed as he slammed against one of the cargo doors, the impact pushing all air out of his lungs. He started making his way, one hand after the other, across the webbing, until his brother grabbed him and pulled him in.

They lay on the floor, Steve on his belly and Jack on his back.

The Hip took a nosedive, piercing the cloudy cover. The cargo bay doors slammed shut.

"Now she'll chew my head off," Steve said, "for not having closed the doors yet."

"You always had a weird taste in women," Jack said, matter-of-factly.

Sandra sat down, the spent tube in her hand, and watched them as they howled with laughter, their laughs lost in the hum of the rotors.

EPILOGUE

Hernan Barreto staggered through the vegetation, hands still tied and a piece of American tape still gagging him. He was lost, his memory a nightmare of stomping dinosaur feet and men shooting and screaming and dying.

He had been inside the cargo hold of Bravo 1 when the chopper had been attacked, and he had crawled out through the madness and the wreckage and the noise.

He did not know where he was anymore.

But he was alive, and that was enough.

A gust of fresh air welcomed him in the clearing, the sky blue above him, the breeze drying the sweat on his chest, causing him to shiver.

He was alive.

He had shown them.

He pulled the tape away, cursing as it pulled off his mustache hair, and then he moved his mouth, stretching the muscles of the cheeks.

He looked down, looking for a sharp stone or something to sever the nylon strip binding his wrists. He kicked through the ferns and the grass.

A chirping sound, and he looked up.

On a stump of a tree in front of him stood a small blue and orange lizard with rainbow scales along the sides. Small round head bent to one side, it observed him.

Hernan grinned and whistled.

The lizard moved up and down on its legs, and whistled back. Another one joined it on its perch.

Hernan heard rustling sounds in the undergrowth.

Small blue and orange lizards. He grinned.

Nothing to worry about.

CHECK OUT OTHER GREAT DINOSAUR THRILLERS

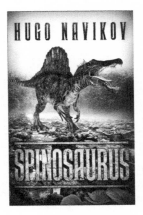

SPINOSAURUS
by Hugo Navikov

Brett Russell is a hunter of the rarest game. His targets are cryptids, animals denied by science. But they are well known by those living on the edges of civilization, where monsters attack and devour their animals and children and lay ruin to their shantytowns.

When a shadowy organization sends Brett to the Congo in search of the legendary dinosaur cryptid Kasai Rex, he will face much more than a terrifying monster from the past.

Spinosaurus is a dinosaur thriller packed with intrigue, action and giant prehistoric predators.

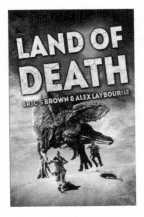

LAND OF DEATH
by Eric S Brown & Alex Laybourne

A group of American soldiers, fleeing an organized attack on their base camp in the Middle East, encounter a storm unlike anything they've seen before. When the storm subsides, they wake up to find themselves no longer in the desert and perhaps not even on Earth. The jungle they've been deposited in is a place ruled by prehistoric creatures long extinct. Each day is a struggle to survive as their ammo begins to run low and virtually everything they encounter, in this land they've been hurled into, is a deadly threat.

CHECK OUT OTHER GREAT DINOSAUR THRILLERS

WRITTEN IN STONE
by David Rhodes

Charles Dawson is trapped 100 million years in the past. Trying to survive from day to day in a world of dinosaurs he devises a plan to change his fate. As he begins to write messages in the soft mud of a nearby stream, he can only hope they will be found by someone who can stop his time travel. Professor Ron Fontana and Professor Ray Taggit, scientists with opposing views, each discover the fossilized messages. While attempting to save Charles, Professor Fontana, his daughter Lauren and their friend Danny are forced to join Taggit and his group of mercenaries. Taggit does not intend to rescue Charles Dawson, but to force Dawson to travel back in time to gather samples for Taggit's fame and fortune. As the two groups jump through time they find they must work together to make it back alive as this fast-paced thriller climaxes at the very moment the age of dinosaurs is ending.

HARD TIME
by Alex Laybourne

Rookie officer Peter Malone and his heavily armed team are sent on a deadly mission to extract a dangerous criminal from a classified prison world. A Kruger Correctional facility where only the hardest, most vicious criminals are sent to fend for themselves, never to return.

But when the team come face to face with ancient beasts from a lost world, their mission is changed. The new objective: Survive.

CHECK OUT OTHER GREAT DINOSAUR THRILLERS

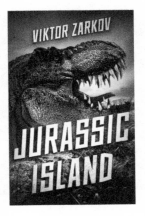

JURASSIC ISLAND
by Viktor Zarkov

Guided by satellite photos and modern technology a ragtag group of survivalists and scientists travel to an uncharted island in the remote South Indian Ocean. Things go to hell in a hurry once the team reaches the island and the massive megalodon that attacked their boats is only the beginning of their desperate fight for survival.

Nothing could have prepared billionaire explorer Joseph Thornton and washed up archaeologist Christopher "Colt" McKinnon for the terrifying prehistoric creatures that wait for them on JURASSIC ISLAND!

K-REX
by L.Z. Hunter

Deep within the Congo jungle, Circuitz Mining employs mercenaries as security for its Coltan mining site. Armed with assault rifles and decades of experience, nothing should go wrong. However, the dangers within the jungle stretch beyond venomous snakes and poisonous spiders. There is more to fear than guerrillas and vicious animals. Undetected, something lurks under the expansive treetop canopy . . .

Something ancient.

Something dangerous.

Kasai Rex!

2083423R00090